TEA AT REID'S

TEA
AT REID'S

Lucy M Currie

JANUS PUBLISHING COMPANY
London, England

First published in Great Britain 1995
by Janus Publishing Company
Edinburgh House, 19 Nassau Street
London W1N 7RE

British Library Cataloguing in Publication Data
A catalogue record for this book is available
from the British Library.

ISBN 1 85756 133 3

Cover design Harold King
Printed and bound in England by
Antony Rowe Ltd, Chippenham, Wiltshire

As this is a purely escapist novel, any resemblance between the characters and living persons would be miraculous. Madeira is a real island but, to one on holiday, it is dreamland.

All unacknowledged poetry quotations and chapter titles are taken from *The Collected Poems of James Elroy Flecker*, edited by J C Squire, published by Martin Secker 1916.

Contents

Chapter 1
Where Empires Sleep

It was reading Paul Scott's *Staying On* that led to Rhoda Brown's holiday in Madeira. A paperback picked up to pass the tedium of a slow train journey was the ultimate cause of Rhoda's second independent holiday. After fifty-five years of life without event and without tragedy, her mother's death had freed her to choose her own destinations. Switzerland had been the first and there she had happened on encounters which had enlarged her understanding of life and human nature. In *Staying On*, Rhoda disliked the characters; there was none of the plain narrative that she enjoyed but the book was still compulsive reading. It was the nostalgic ambience that had gripped her. Like the Roman twilight in Britain, there was the pathos of surviving a period of apparent distinction, the monotony of the routine of living in the place, of being even on the fringe of great events. There was the atmosphere of a mysterious failure which she associated with her long-dead father.

The lights had gone out for Captain Brown as they had for Europe in 1914 and, though he had survived the war, it was to him an alien world. Home and education had given him the religious and patriotic ideas of Newbolt. The breathless hush of the cricket match and the thin red line defending Christian civilisation were for him genuine experiences recollected in tranquillity. He had been one of Kelly's contingent at the relief of Fort Chitral in 1895 when frostbite and a bullet wound had combined to cut short his army career. Ten years later he married the debutante Lady Alexandra Cheviot – an attraction of opposites. Handsome, lively and extrovert, the hard

1

gaiety of the Edwardian decade suited her. Both their worlds were destroyed by the 1914–1918 war. The disability he had suffered in the Afghan Campaign prevented Captain Brown from seeing active service. He endured a War Office job in the deepening shadows of European corruption and decay.

Many years after his marriage, Rhoda was born. Captain Brown welcomed a daughter for, though he had a fine heritage to leave a son, he could see the twentieth century would deny him any true enjoyment of it. Rhoda was four when her father died yet he seemed to influence her more than her mother. Her mother's dominating character had dictated Rhoda's everyday life but it was the father, revealed after her mother's death in the clearing up of long forgotten papers and souvenirs, that guided the new era of her life. Her father's addiction to mountaineering in Switzerland had led to her first adventure. Now the recollection that he had spent some time in Madeira on his return from India in the last years of Queen Victoria's reign came to her. He had kept a diary during his stay spent, inevitably in that period, at Reid's Hotel. Madeira must always have had for the British an aura of 'staying on'. Its visitors, en route for 'home' for the last time would find there a spurious importance unlike the inevitable decline into the ancient mariner reminiscences at Cheltenham or Budleigh Salterton that produced the cliché 'When I was in Poona in . . .' Her father's diary of that period had been of no great interest to her when she had first skipped through it, though she recalled the mention of the governor who had given Napoleon a cask of madeira wine and the title of 'His Majesty' on the way into exile on St Helena. Perhaps the physical background of the island would shed more light on the personality of her little-known father if she read the story of that long-ago time on the scene. She made up her mind. She, too, would have tea at Reid's.

2

Chapter 2
Gods Who Take Vengeance

Rhoda suspected that, in spite of his involvement in the siege of Chitral, her father lacked the spirit of heroic adventure that at least Ethel M Dell saw in the Indian army of his day. Lady Alexandra had always preferred to be the big fish in a small pond and had stuck to insular life. So it was probably heredity that led Rhoda to a travel agent to provide the quickest and easiest way of reaching, and staying in, Madeira – a package tour.

Arriving early at the airport, she bestowed her case in the 'Left Luggage' and provided herself with a continental breakfast. Surprised to find herself alone in a complete section of the restaurant, she realised she was in the smokers' area. Alone, she was able to enjoy a privilege battled for by the American-type anti-smokers pressure group, though as she did so she sighed for the briefly past day when an individual could bring influence to bear in Britain. However, for her a holiday was a newly found way of escape from reality so she turned to the leisurely enjoyment of coffee and rolls with the knowledge that she could still get first choice of seats by arriving at the checkout as it opened.

In due course she ambled back to the 'Left Luggage' only to discover she had lost her ticket. In crimson confusion she opened each purse and container in her handbag though realising she had probably automatically dropped her ticket in a litter bin on her way to the restaurant. As the queue lengthened behind her the attendant wearily suggested that she should fill in a form, while the wise virgins behind her produced their tickets glancing at her with

3

expressions ranging from pity to contemptuous malice. The last restored Rhoda's fighting spirit and with an icy flash of blue eyes which could surprise her friends she ensured a hasty aversion of eyes and wrote her address – Half Acre, Stoneborough, Barsetshire. Her new home had been built in the kitchen garden of her father's estate which had been absorbed by a new department in the University of Stoneborough. She had thus escaped becoming part of an urban developer's tight-fisted sprawl and achieved a residence both new and unique. She often wondered whether she would otherwise have resorted to the contemporary fashion of buying an old barn or a deconsecrated church to achieve domiciliary distinction. Now at least the consciousness of a place uniquely hers restored her aplomb and enabled her to receive calmly the case handed to her by the attendant duly authorised by his bureaucratic superior.

Now she could check in but, alas, too late for the comparatively comfortable gangway seat. She had to accept a middle seat and was wedged in front and sides for the next three or four hours. Discomfort, like the prospect of death, concentrates the mind wonderfully and Rhoda decided on total withdrawal hoping that her choice of paperback would be as happy as the one responsible for this uncomfortable journey. It wasn't.

Rhoda was conscious of penetrating voices behind her, sometimes separate, sometimes in chorus. Evidently both were determined talkers with no concept of conversation. It became impossible not to listen.

'My eldest daughter is quite a friend of Princess Anne, you know.'

'Top consultant – used to fly out a lot to the Gulf states but the money's moved away now.'

'Where?'

'Well not so much anywhere but with all the insurance companies behind private medicine he does pretty well at home.'

'My son's in computers – very talented, twenty thousand a year at twenty and already doubled.'

'Met her at Badminton. I encouraged her to ride – not up to Olympic standards but next best. Money's everywhere so royalty's the only inner circle now. Difficult to get into unless you know one who's gone off the rails.'

'Could walk into Harrods and buy any suit he wanted within a year of leaving school – didn't bother with university. Ah! lunch coming up.'

One merit of the pair was they did not talk with their mouths full so the hot lunch gave a brief hearing space. Her companions to the right and left had fallen asleep and seemed very little more conscious when they were awake. After a second cup of coffee Rhoda sat on, now further wedged in front with the tray and no hope of movement so she bestowed a glance on her neighbours fallen into what seemed their natural state of inertia. Though with no personal resemblance, they might have been twins. The thirtyish woman by the window wore a jump suit of such superior cut and design as to bear no relation to Rhoda's acquisition from her local boutique. The man at the gangway was equally well clad yet equally anonymous. Rhoda tried to decide the cause of this phenomenon and decided that, though both had quite good features, their lack of expression deprived them of individuality. Like the shrill passenger's son in computers they probably spent their time making money until they became as indistinguishable as the credit cards they lived by and for. They appeared to have no connection with one another yet Rhoda wondered why they had failed to get the front seats. Possibly the fact that the occupants were all disabled in one way or another had prevented them from asserting their financial power.

In time the trays disappeared, the time for landing drew near and Rhoda looked forward to human society again. It was not to be. After two attempts the pilot regretfully announced that the runway was immersed in cloud and the plane must go to Porto Santo till the runway was clear. Within a few minutes they had landed, ominously beside another stationary aircraft. Here they lurked for what seemed eternity but could only have been a couple of hours as the light was beginning to fade. Again the omnipotent voice from above (Rhoda with mild blasphemy, felt like Moses receiving orders from on high which he didn't want to hear). They could not land and must go to the mainland of Portugal and spend the night there. And so the Promised Land retreated and, like Moses, Rhoda prepared for another spell in the desert.

It turned out to be a very comfortable hotel. A literally fishy dinner was consumed in the company of several couples, courteous but avoiding sociability with Rhoda lest an unwanted single should become attached to the Ark society that enters two by two into package holidays. Rhoda, who preferred the privileges of solitude to fifth-wheeling withdrew as soon as possible to her room. To her

5

delighted astonishment it proved to be a genuine single – a single bed with all other furniture and facilities of full size. Preparations for the night proceeded apace with no extra beds to negotiate and she made a mental note of the name of the hotel chain but without much hope that it would be an extensive one.

Next morning the hotel dissipated all the well earned goodwill of the night before by not serving breakfast till 7.45 when the coach was due to leave at 8.00. Rhoda, unhindered by sociability, took her coffee and rolls to a far window where she had an excellent view of harbour and mud flats, her first experience of the Algarve.

Inevitably the departure of the coach was delayed half an hour giving Rhoda time to walk round the harbour, consciously enjoying the open air after yesterday's confinement in the plane. It was the bliss of solitude. She would meet no one she knew, no one for whom she felt any responsibility.

She sat down for a few minutes and idly watched the scene. Looking incongruous in the quiet early morning were the two smart passengers who had sat beside her on the plane. They were carrying briefcases and as they passed one another the briefcases changed hands. It struck Rhoda as strange as they had not appeared to be acquainted on the plane. Her imagination took flight. Mafia? Spies? Industrial secrets? She abandoned the idiocies of contemporary civilisation and withdrew into enjoyment of sunlight and scenery, so successfully that she had to walk rapidly back to the hotel where the coach was now standing.

Portugal 'done', the passengers re-embarked and without further untoward incident finally bumped down in Madeira.

Chapter 3
Good Human Music

Entranced by the flowers and shrubs blooming everywhere along the way, Rhoda took little note of the acute angles of the road though subconsciously deciding not to hire a car on the island. She saw the two persistent talkers in the front of the coach still pursuing their monologues. The smart pair (or separates?) were also there and most of the others were couples enjoying the advantages of retirement in an affluent society. They were dropped off in groups at the five star hotels which provided comfort and service with all the problems of life tucked out of sight – or nearly. Alone in a handsome room, the sun shining on the balcony, Rhoda relaxed.

Inevitably, Rhoda's thoughts in her new surroundings found expression in poetry. She had learned by heart much of nineteenth-century verse under the direction of her governess and had absorbed more from her own reading throughout her life. Some lines seemed applicable, to her own pilgrimage.

> We are the pilgrims, master; we shall
>   go
> Always a little further: it may be
> Beyond that last blue mountain, barred
>   with snow
> Across that angry or that glimmering sea,
>
> White on a throne or guarded in a cave
> There lives a prophet who can understand.

7

Flecker's lines recalled the basic conception of the Arthurian legend, repeated in many cultures, a concept that made her life worth living. Somewhere in the universe, being made sense, a belief that enabled the dreamer to avoid being crushed by the realities of everyday life.

The established Church of England had always been the outward and visible sign of eternal realities to Rhoda. Two days after her arrival was Sunday so she made her way to the English church. Here again she would be sharing an experience with her father. Firmly set in the 1662 Prayer Book, she could be sure of Cranmer's timeless prose though *Hymns Ancient and Modern* was probably still an objectionably modern innovation in the last years of the nineteenth century.

She was surprised to see a young clergyman enter robed at eleven o'clock. She had expected that this living would be occupied by a retired man ordained in the 1928 Prayer Book Revision period. This haggard cleric could not be more than in his mid-thirties and looked the type who should be battling with inner city decay and a population brought up with not even a slender attachment to the Anglican tradition. She was to learn her guess was exact. The Rev Barnabas Roscommon had built a church in a derelict area of Manchester – 'a temple not made with hands'. He had firmly resisted any attempt to erect another building at a time when redundant church buildings were being everywhere deconsecrated to become novel offices or residences or demolished to provide more dereliction in areas which already had too much. His church was a small, slowly acquired band of converts from total secularism. Hope of real life had penetrated a few with whom he had battled for a tenants' association, restored housing, the possibility of pride in a home. He had succeeded at the cost of physical collapse and barely escaped mental breakdown. A cleric, no more than a layman, can live by a faith that is humanly speaking all demands and no rewards.

An observant bishop had stepped in in time to save him from total collapse. In Madeira there was neither need nor wish for innovation. His clerical duty was clear. Even hospital duty was comparatively easy, dealing more with the natural approach of death to the aged instead of with young lives destroyed by unemployment, alcohol, drugs or violence. For him this ministry was almost an escape from the unnatural realities of urban poverty in the midst of indifferent affluence.

Rhoda had noticed the entry of a young woman with three children, two identical boys of about seven and a girl several years younger. Their impeccable behaviour indicated early acquaintance with worship and the accepted obligation of a rectory family not to annoy the congregation. They had evidently adapted a play ritual of the normal imitation of adults that lies behind many childhood games. The boys found places in prayer and hymn books and showed them to the sister until she suddenly sat down and, falling asleep, was seen and heard no more till the end of the service.

Rhoda was pleasantly surprised by the sermon. Instead of a trumpet blast against a seemingly comfortable and affluent congregation, there was a coherent exposition of the gospel for the day with an implicit appeal to continue in such well doing as was within the powers and situation of his hearers. Rhoda gave the young clergyman credit for intelligent Christian humanism in forgetting his own priorities to forward the pastoral needs of this, to him, alien group. Selecting, according to her custom, one practical point for herself, she accepted a call to look out for opportunities of hospitality – a comfortable hotel and well filled purse giving her the obvious qualifications for response to the call to 'be not forgetful to entertain strangers'.

The service over, Rhoda moved slowly down the aisle and emerged beside two women she had seen together at the hotel. One large and expansive, immediately introduced herself by the unlikely name of Pixie Putley. Rhoda murmured her own name and Miss Putley introduced her tall, thin friend, Constance de Lisle. Mrs de Lisle was very unlike her companion. She looked as if her nose was raised permanently to avoid an unpleasant smell, probably foreigners, and her appearance was so totally correct as to combine distinction with nullity. Rhoda could visualise Pixie Putley running all the voluntary organisations of a village and overriding personality clashes by the force of her own good nature. Constance de Lisle must be a handicap which Pixie assumed to complement her gregarious nature. She was a friend of all the world and swept Rhoda along with them to the drink and chat which followed the service in the church garden. Mrs de Lisle, having decided that Rhoda was one of her own kind, lowered her nose after removing her glance from a dark, intense-looking woman with a mongrel hair style, and said,

'This reminds me of the rectory garden parties to raise money for the organ fund. Everyone was invited.'

Ignoring the implication that the lower orders should have known better than to accept the invitation, Rhoda replied,

'Yes, indeed. They were delightful occasions.'

Mrs de Lisle looked at her suspiciously.

'You *like* mixed gatherings!'

'I like meeting people without the obligations of intimacy.'

'Ah!' Mrs de Lisle was satisfied assuming Rhoda meant what *she* thought and unable to imagine that Rhoda would not wish to have the privilege of closer acquaintance with *her*. Fortunately she now noticed a resident whom she believed to be of her own class and Rhoda was left without the strain of concocting more *double entendres*.

She was wedged for the moment by the stone commemorating the origins of the long-lasting alliance between Britain and Portugal. She took the opportunity of such close quarters to read the inscription to Philippa of Lancaster, daughter of John of Gaunt, aunt of Henry V and mother of Henry the Navigator. Rhoda thought of Nigel Cooper, a bitter young social science lecturer she had met in Switzerland. How he would have envied anyone with such influential connections. But what extraordinary lives the women of medieval royalty were compelled to live. Still Philippa was one who made her mark at the inauguration of the golden age of Portugese navigation.

The disintegration of the nearest group opened up a space and Rhoda was able to move to a seat occupied by a couple in the fortyish age group. They proved to be at leisure owing to the husband's redundancy. His wife had given up her job to come with him to Madeira where he was acting as a consultant. Presumably his handshake had been a solid silver if not a gold one.

Rhoda wondered at the readiness with which people disclosed their business in the holiday atmosphere, recognising that she shared the tendency, offering her Christian name in a way she would not have done in England.

'Frank and Harriet Grantley,' responded Mrs Grantley. 'We've taken an apartment as we expect to be here for some months. We are trying to learn the language and finding it very difficult.'

10

'I'm not surprised. I find it difficult to isolate recognisable sounds sufficiently to tell whether people are speaking Portuguese or some other tongue unknown to me.'

'Harry has a better ear than I,' said Harriet, 'and more incentive as he hopes to start a second career here.'

'And would you like to live in Madeira?'

'Frank would and I'm prepared to try it!'

'The pace is slower than anywhere else in the west,' said Frank. 'I don't care for cut-throat competition.'

Rhoda looked at him and saw lines of fatigue as well as humour on his face. He seemed kindly and that was not an attribute which would help him in dealing with business where aggression was valued above honesty. He probably had lost his job from working on the assumption that there are other objectives besides financial profit.

Harriet glanced rather anxiously at her husband and said,

'The pace is certainly slower. I went into the chemist's the other day to get a shampoo. I brought the old bottle in the hope of getting a replacement of the same make. The assistant looked at it and said that they did not stock it. Just then a middle-aged Portuguese woman approached the counter and the assistant, recognising a friend, moved along to shake hands with her and an animated conversation ensued. As I wished to ask for the nearest approach to my shampoo that they did stock, I waited and sure enough after some minutes the friend departed and the assistant moved back in front of me.'

'We have another make but the perfume is different.'

I asked to see it. The perfume was certainly different and so strong that I flinched. I was about to say it was too powerful for me when a young woman with a bonny baby came in and I was again deserted. The baby was duly admired and I noted the frequent recurrence of the "sh" sound in Portuguese. I began to wonder if they were discussing a lullaby. Eventually the man took something from the shelf, handed it to the mother and turned to me again. He removed the odorous shampoo from my outstretched hand and walked off. I assumed the transaction was now at an end and was turning away when he returned with another bottle.

'This is very good but very expensive,' he said and, after giving me a chance to read the price appeared to be about to remove it

11

immediately. I hung on in order to smell it and found out thereby the reason why it was so expensive.

'I'll have it,' I said.

The assistant looked astonished. Evidently he expected English visitors to be interested only in bargains. He took it from me and I thought for a moment he was about to restore it to the shelf for another acquaintance expected any minute. But no. The bottle was wrapped and I paid for it without further interruption. I had spent twenty minutes on the purchase but I had enjoyed free human drama without the trauma of fearing I should find a parking ticket on my car.'

'The combination of leisurely work with good humour is the great attraction here,' said Rhoda. 'Every activity becomes the sort of human drama one saw on the stage before the kitchen-sink era and the American discovery that they could shock their respectable public by printing four-letter words and saying them in the theatre. Twenty years later we are still enduring the language and outlook on sex and violence of would-be naughty nine year olds. Here, I suppose, poverty has compelled people to grow up and the church has kept family life alive. You still see older children playing protectively with younger ones and whole families, including adolescents, walking together.'

'I wonder if that's what makes for good service in hotels,' continued Frank. 'If the various teams all belong to the same family, they are accustomed to one another and don't waste time on arguments no one is going to win.'

'I believe you're right.' Rhoda recalled watching a team of waiters in the hotel the day before. 'All the routine of life is invested with communal drama. Yesterday three waiters arrived to lay the cloth on a long table. Correctly dressed as to black trousers, they were topped with somewhat déshabillé shirts. A minuet ensued as they backed and filled to get the cloth flat on the table. A long dialogue with much gesticulation followed. Was there a wrinkle in the cloth? Whatever the fault, the waiters repeated the dance – the cloth was relaid. A decoration was placed at one end. A blue jacketed superior moved off but another character arrived. The maître d'hotel? Now the drama reaches concert pitch. With the bravura of the conductor of an orchestra reaching crescendo his hands flew hither and thither. The waiters stood attentive. Blue Jacket re-appeared. More gesticulation, more dialogue. The maître d'hotel swept the cloth off the table and vanished. Blue Jacket shrugged and addressed the waiters who in turn offered comments. They relaid the cloth. Blue Jacket disappeared. All semblance of activity ceased. The waiters, with nods and shrugs, took their turn in debating the preceding drama. They moved the decoration a few inches to the right, then returned it to what seemed to have been its original place. Then they withdrew in contemplation of their work. The coloured jackets had totally withdrawn. The white shirts relaxed into personal gossip.'

Rhoda became aware of Frank and Harriet noiselessly clapping their hands and realised she had been carried away, reliving one of the little dramas which had not only enlivened the work of the hotel staff but also entertained the guests. She laughed at herself but stuck to her guns in the assurance that the Portuguese had retained a lively humanity lost to other nationalities, who were racing to technological anonymity in preparation for the twenty-first century which they would probably never live to see.

'I admire people who are prepared to live *now*.'

Frank admitted that the weeks since her had arrived in Madeira had been more enjoyable than the best of his working life.

Harriet added, 'We are hoping the children may find jobs here when they are finished with university.' Rhoda politely enquired after their interests and found one, the son, was reading law while the girl was specialising in the history of art.

The crowd around them had diminished and with the usual, 'Hope to see you again,' they were about to part when Rhoda became aware of Pixie Putley hovering near. Rhoda looked towards her and introduced Frank and Harriet Grantley. After an exchange of conventional greetings Pixie said, 'Hope to meet you again' to the Grantleys and to Rhoda, 'Constance and I have a taxi back to the hotel. Would you like to join us?'

Rhoda accepted gratefully having become aware on the way to church that her shoes were unsuited to cobbled streets and erratic paving, though her gratitude was tempered by the fact that an invitation to lunch with the two friends would ensue. Not that she disliked either of them – no one could dislike Pixie – and Constance de Lisle was interesting as a social dinosaur, but for the present she had really had enough of people. However when the suggestion of lunch came, she agreed and they stopped at a noted seafood restaurant. Rhoda had never understood why fish had to be called seafood in a restaurant. Perhaps the intention was to dissociate it from the stink of the fish market and to present it to the imagination in an aura (or odour) of maritime glamour.

The conversation naturally ran on the encounters of the morning. Constance de Lisle had discovered that the Rev Barnabas Roscommon was one of the Roscommons of Tayside, so the good behaviour of the children was remarked on rather than his extraordinary predilection for the Down if not Out.

'Always their own fault,' Mrs de Lisle remarked, 'they will marry young and have children they can't afford.'

'Well, it's natural to want their own homes,' said Pixie bracingly and Constance, used to this plug in her condemnations of human nature turned to Mrs Roscommon, who also came of a 'good family' – their virtue lying in having held on to the world's goods consistently for a number of generations. Still Rhoda thought 'good' might be used in its true sense of the cleric's wife, as she had been prepared to sacrifice the benefits of wealth to support her husband's chosen work.

Even Pixie could find nothing to say of a young woman whom Rhoda identified as the one with the mongrel hair style.

'She's one of those who pride themselves on their rudeness,' Pixie said. 'Convention may have been overdone in the old days but to contradict everything one says on first acquaintance is carrying so-called frankness too far.'

Rhoda, noting Constance's expression of disgust, mischievously enquired the topic of conversation. At this Pixie laughed heartily and, good-naturedly mimicking her efforts, reproduced the dialogue.

' "What a lovely garden, isn't it?" '

' "No, very ordinary compared with Blandy's or even St Catherine's." '

' "Yes, of course they're wonderful but this is a pleasant spot for a neighbourly gathering." '

' "Not much neighbourliness in charging for a cup of coffee." '

' "Oh, but such a good cause and it brings people together." '

' "Better apart, most of them." '

(Rhoda wondered if Constance de Lisle had appeared at this point.)

' "How do you like Madeira?" '

' "It's all right." '

' "Perhaps we shall meet again on one of the excursions." '

'She muttered in reply something that sounded like, "Not if I know it." I'll give her the benefit of the doubt over the actual words but the intent was certainly negative.'

'What extraordinary people are found in Church of England congregations nowadays,' Mrs de Lisle exclaimed. 'Surely that type would be more at home in a gospel hall.'

Rhoda contemplated commenting that Jesus would have felt at home in both but decided it might be considered blasphemy, or worse, bad taste. Moreover, Pixie would be distressed by the implied criticism of her friend by a stranger, so instead she described her encounter with the Grantleys whom Pixie would like and Constance would consider 'worthy' people.

Altogether the meal provided more agreeable companionship than Rhoda had expected. Her own passion for solitude responded to something in the exclusiveness of Constance de Lisle and her detached interest in humanity delighted in the radiant interest in everything and everybody that Pixie exuded. Still it was restful to find herself back in her room with the option of being alone for the rest of the day. She hunted out her father's diary and retired to the balcony with a view to planning her activities on the basis of what she read there.

Chapter 4
The Land Beyond the Door

Reid's Hotel

7 January
We landed two days ago. The relief of the mild climate is great, but
I still feel worn out. I cannot forget the men suffering from snow
blindness mown down by the tribesmen they could hardly see.
Then attacking the fort exhausted after descending ravines on
improvised rope ladders and climbing steep slippery goat tracks.
Worst of all were the mine-blasted bodies of both sides. Still, the
Empire stands only by such work. I shall be glad to resign my
commission and retire to country life. I look forward to getting to
England in April. Browning knew what he was talking about:

> The chaffinch sings on the orchard bough
> In England.

There seem to be nothing but sea birds here – unattractive creatures
compared with our wrens and robins. I find it difficult to move
about so this diary will provide an occupation. Madeira has an
interesting past not least its long standing alliance with England.
Napoleon put in here on his way to St Helena and the governor
lost his posting for addressing him as 'Your Majesty' instead of
'General' – always damned punctilious about minutiae that don't
matter at the Foreign Office. Courtesy to a defeated foe hurts no
one. It's said they deprived him of everything he possessed but he

16

must have been a broken man after Waterloo. Why did he take on the Russians? That climate would defeat anyone. Still the British have kept their hold on India in spite of the climate. We've lost a lot of good men though. If they had lived they might in later life have manned the Foreign Office and kept the Queen informed. There wouldn't be so many Chitrals if there had been any understanding at home. Communication is too slow and you always get men on the spot who are afraid to act on their own initiative, 'marking time to earn his KCB', as Kipling wrote. Strange fellow that but he can write. I'm rambling on but feel better. Perhaps I shall go out tomorrow. This new hotel is very comfortable but the contrast between the chintzy drawing-room and the Afghan mountain passes is too great as yet. I must get Chitral out of my head.

10 January
Decidedly better. I have had tea on the terrace at Reid's. I prefer the countryside but there is something about a view of unlimited sea that evokes feelings of eternity. Would it have been better to end in the Malakand Pass than remain to the day-to-day tedium of an uneventful life keeping keepers up to the mark and losing money on the land?

12 January
I went to the English church yesterday. It was like home to hear the service in traditional language. I had lunch with the chaplain afterwards. Apparently Napoleon was not stripped of all his money, for some gold louis with which he paid the governor for supplies were buried in the foundation of the church. He thought his family would want and be allowed to visit him, especially his favourite sister, Pauline, whose expenditure on entertainments had aroused some feeling among the local population of Elba. There was a tradition that he left an elaborately carved box with the governor as a gift for her if she were prevented from proceeding further than Madeira. After his death the box was presented to the church and is now used for the Communion Vessels in the Visitation of the Sick. It had certainly contained one of those busts of Napoleon in which his sister, Elisa, Grand Duchess of Tuscany, astutely established a profitable trade. The bust came to light at the time of the Third Empire and was presented to the then chaplain who discreetly

17

placed it in an obscure niche in the church gallery. The chaplain, who was interested in the local legends arising from the storm that coincided with the *Northumberland* putting in at Madeira showed the bust to me – an undistinguished piece of work but I understand that the duchess had them mass produced – an extraordinary family.

19 January
Have had a relapse. A good deal of pain and depression. However I had tea on the terrace again today and still hope to be back home in April. The chaplain called with Communion. Afterwards he showed me the box reputedly Napoleon's. It is heavy at the base and quite large enough to have contained the small bust I saw in the church. It was ingeniously divided to contain the vessels and a wicker-work container had been constructed for safe carriage – rather cumbersome but I suppose worth using for the historical interest.

25 January
Better again. I went to the British Club today and met Colonel Seaton, who settled in Madeira after retiring recently. His wife died just before his retirement and he thought life would be better here with no associations to remind him of their plans together. It's easier to deal with the mechanics of living too – cheap domestic help and a mild climate providing some of the benefits without the snags of service in India. He's worried about a son who's turned out badly, not surprisingly with no settled home life. He was sent home from India to save his life as a small child but it wasn't much of a life. He was at several sorts of boarding school in term time as he grew up and went to various relations who didn't particularly want him for the holidays. He refused to try for Sandhurst, went up to Oxford, got into debt and came down without a degree. He is to stay here for a while. I doubt whether either of them will enjoy the visit.

1 February
Decidedly better. I have been reading about a visit to Madeira in the last decade – a lady called Ellen Taylor. She seems to have been an acute observer. Commenting on the natives she says, 'Their faces were very prepossessing and their manner gentle and courteous.' That agrees with my observation. One cannot imagine them

involved in the sort of labour troubles England has endured in the present century. Of course the main occupation is agriculture – very hard work in this hilly country. They have no distractions as it is almost impossible for most of them to reach the coast. They have a wonderful irrigation system – *levadas*, which provides tourists with the recreation of walking in remote spots. I went with Colonel Seaton and his son Alexander. I think both were glad of the presence of a comparative stranger. Alexander is a good-looking young man – takes after his father in that respect but not in any other. He has a shifty way of looking at you to see if what he says is approved and if he thinks not he modifies or contradicts what he's said. He seems afraid of his father and that exasperates the colonel. I wished we had made up a larger party as it was uncomfortable mediating between the two. I would have liked to be alone to enjoy the trees and plants many of which are blooming even at this time of year. I think I can be sure of getting home to a second spring in April. I imagine the colonel hoped young Seaton and I would take to each other and I would provide safe company of his own age but our lives have been so different that we have nothing in common. I've had the discipline and responsibility of an army officer. Seaton seems to have spent his life evading authority and indulging in questionable pleasures. We did chat a bit about Napoleon's association with the island but, as he expressed great admiration for Napoleon as compared to Wellington, he annoyed the colonel without impressing me. I will try to see more of him as the two are better apart and there are not many young men at Reid's.

5 February
To quote Ellen Taylor again, 'Instead of tiring of the quiet, simple life we lead, we seem to enjoy it more and more.' Of course returning health has much to do with the feeling and I have made several agreeable acquaintances at the British Club. I have been there with young Seaton but he does not improve on acquaintance. He left me to pay the bill although the colonel had provided him with money for the purpose but he evidently preferred to increase his allowance at my expense. Poor devil, marred in the making.' He'll never be able to stand on his own feet in Madeira or anywhere else. But he is the only fly in the ointment. The days go by pleasantly in warmth and sunshine and the horrors of Chitral have receded. I suppose the thought of death from my injuries caused me to exaggerate

19

them. After all war is the only means of establishing peace and justice among the uncivilised and the British have the mission to do it. What would have happened to classical culture and the Pax Romana without the disciplined armies? Why ask? The Fall of Rome introduced the Dark Ages. Chitral is one small bulwark against the collapse of our empire. Alex Seaton was arguing against my view yesterday (he never ventures to when the colonel is present), pointing out the short-lived existence of Napoleon's power in spite of his military genius. He has become very interested, almost obsessed, with Napoleon's brief association with Madeira. Burying the gold louis in the foundation of the church seemed a waste to him. I fear Christian education has washed lightly over him. An alabaster box of ointment would be as senseless to him as to Judas. Yet even Judas was sickened by the gold pieces for his betrayal. Perhaps Seaton can be turned to better values. He seems to think that Napoleon must have hidden treasure on his way to St Helena to use for another attempt to return to power but the ill health that dogged his exile prevented his retrieving it, and where else but Madeira could he have left it? I suppose it is possible but if so it would have come to light by now or been used if it had been discovered. When I said this, Seaton pointed out that after thousands of years, in spite of constant looting, treasures were now being found in Egyptian tombs. Poor chap. He is obsessed with the desire for money to get free from his father's authority but he hasn't the talent or the determination to earn it. He has already tried to borrow from me but I have refused to go behind the colonel's back. Alex always leaves me to pay the bill when we go out together and that is as far as I am willing to finance him. I doubt whether anyone can help him. He is as weak as water and his imagination is such that he loses touch with reality.

12 February
I have neglected Seaton for more congenial company lately so today I invited him to join me in a toboggan ride which seems to be a favourite expedition among visitors to the island. I was rather annoyed with the colonel who virtually ordered Alex to go with me. I suppose it is impossible for an officer to lose the 'Go and he goeth' attitude but it is not a good one in family life. I could not withdraw my invitation but Alex was sulky and I would have enjoyed it more on my own. But, as Ellen Taylor wrote, 'Very

20

delightful is the sensation of this rapid rushing through the air.' It brought back Christmas holidays of my boyhood. The hills outside Stoneborough provided grand toboggan tracks and the snow a less bumpy ride than the cobbles here. Though a bit shaken up I was cheered to feel none the worse for the jolting and it cured Alex of the sulks for today. We dropped in at the British Club before going back to Reid's and had drinks on the terrace with Major and Mrs Alderton who are here on leave for few a weeks before going on to England. We were interested in the tree, about ten or twelve years old, planted just in front of the terrace. I wondered how long it would outlive all those of us now looking at it. Does man's consciousness compensate for being so long outlived by the buildings he raises and the trees he plants? My mind wandered as Alex tried to shock the major and his wife with more way out ideas. But the major has plenty of experience of subaltern silliness and, in the euphoria of leave, merely laughed while Mrs Alderton listened kindly. She doesn't care much for the colonel and has a mother's sympathy for the lack of home life of 'Indian' children and after a time he began to talk more sensibly to Mrs Alderton while the Major and I strolled around the grounds. The major is interested in natural history and we conversed about Darwin and his theories. He suggested joining me next time I took a walk on the *levadas* and I agreed with pleasure. If Mrs Alderton comes too it should be considerably pleasanter than the one with the colonel and Alex. She will accompany Seaton while the Major and I can enjoy the attractions of nature. Selfish of me but I've had too much of Seaton and Mrs Alderton seems to like him. He is probably at his best with motherly women after the extreme authoritarianism of his father.

18 February
We went to a village where the square is used for football. It is difficult to find enough level ground for a pitch here but the British managed to introduce football. Football and cricket are the exports of the empire. I wonder if competition outweighs the benefits of team games. I foresee a time when it may lead to trouble. Alex Seaton was with me. I cannot shake him off. I would prefer to be alone more now that I feel comparatively well but whether to please his father or because he can't bear solitude I find I have to plan discreetly to avoid him. I am very interested in the history of the

21

island but Seaton seems to care only about Napoleon's visit. He cross-examined me about what the chaplain told me of how the bust of Napoleon was preserved in the church gallery. I can't think why he doesn't ask the chaplain himself as he has to go to church with his father but I suppose that's the trouble. He is afraid to take any initiative when the colonel is present. He still makes a confidante of Mrs Alderton but they are leaving for home soon.

20 February
A most extraordinary thing has happened. An attempt has been made to break into the church. Such sacrilege has never been known here yet I suppose it must have been one of the natives. It is most unlike them but all peoples have their rotten apples and this one must have hoped to get access to the collections. No precautions are taken against thieves except for locking doors and I expect the locks are not unique. The fellow was interrupted owing to an exceptional noise of dogs barking which eventually brought out several people to drive them off and it is thought the thief made his escape in the confusion. Stray dogs are a pest in Madeira. Like the rabbits in Australia they were brought in with the best intentions but foreigners have no idea how to look after animals. I'm looking forward to a welcome home from Shag and Shad but they are well trained and have a purpose in life being sheep dogs. I digress. Nothing was taken from the church but the thief had definitely made an entry and oddly enough had made for the gallery, where he had knocked over a pile of hymn books presumably in his rush to escape when he heard the furore outside. Anyway it is providing a new topic of conversation among visitors, especially those who have not the energy for *levada* walks or toboggan rides. People still come here for their health but I think no longer believe the climate is of help for consumption – too damp and humid. A lot of people used to come for that reason judging by the monuments in the British cemetery. I was struck there with the eighteenth-century style of the memorials. Everything here seems to belong to an earlier generation than ours. A girl of 18 who died in 1839 is thus commemorated:

Christina MacDowell gave early indications of decided piety. To the close of her short life, she sustained her Christian profession with much meekness and wisdom; and, when cut off by pulmonary ailment, as mourning survivors are tempted to think too soon for them, though seasonably for her, she exemplified the resignation and peacefulness of falling asleep in Jesus.

A Victorian sentiment enshrined in eighteenth-century periods.

27 February

Gossip about the felonious entry into the church has died down as rumours that the state of the queen's health is precarious are being circulated. They have increased of late as is natural at Her Majesty's advanced age but I trust they are ill founded as I fear her death would usher in many undesirable changes that her presence, however frail, holds back. I have had no further relapses and though lacking in energy believe my health to be improving steadily and I can look forward to seeing an English spring again. It will be strange to go home to a second spring for here it is warm enough to sit in the sunshine out of doors and the gardens do not lack colourful flowers. Young Seaton has not been hanging around so much in the last week. He seems nervous and depressed – I suppose he sees no way of escape from his father's authority and indeed I pity them both. There can be no happy future for them together.

10 March

Colonel Seaton and I lunched today at the house of one of the English residents whose grandfather settled in Madeira after being stationed here during the Napoleonic wars. The colonel comes from a long line with a military tradition and his grandfather had been acquainted with the Gordons' grandfather before he settled in Madeira. The connection had been discovered in conversation at the British Club – hence the invitation. I was invited as a friend of young Seaton and would have enjoyed the occasion very much for the view over Funchal Bay from the Gordons' house is glorious but Alex dragged in his King Charles's head to the annoyance of the colonel though Mr Gordon enjoyed telling some anecdotes about his grandfather's experiences with the occupying garrison. This did not satisfy Alex who, with more persistence than courtesy, continued with questions about Napoleon's visit and his communications with the then governor long after it was clear that he was boring his company. Fortunately the party broke up to view the Gordons' garden and the colonel and I walked with Mr Gordon while Seaton continued to bore Mrs Gordon. The garden is delightful, the uneven terrain, inevitable in Madeira, having enabled the owners to mass blooms at different levels to great effect. Hearing that I had extensive pleasure grounds at Stoneborough Grange, Mr Gordon promised to have ready various cuttings and plants for me to take back with me when I sailed home and I look forward to improving the borders and shrubberies as far as Macpherson, my head gardener, will permit.

16 March

My passage home is booked and three weeks today I sail for home. I still tire too easily and fear I may never lose a limp but as I am as fit as I can expect to be I must not delay returning to the duties on my estate too long. I could enjoy the carefree life here only too much but without my military profession I cannot accept a life of idleness. Alex Seaton is a warning against falling into an aimless existence and his father has at last recognised that keeping him on the island is doing no good. He is using his influence with the Gordons to try to get his son a subordinate post in their branch in London, in the hope that a daily routine will keep him out of mischief. He has therefore booked Seaton's passage on the ship I am taking and has asked me to continue to befriend his son. I pointed out that Stoneborough is a long way from London and that I had no town house to encourage visits to the capital but, seeing the despair he felt, I promised to do anything I could to keep Alex on the straight and narrow. I do go to stay at my club occasionally and shall try to fulfil my promise by inviting Seaton to dinner when I am there but I don't believe he will last long in a steady job. Since he has learned he is to go home on the same boat as I he has been inclined to avoid me here. I am glad of it as I shall enjoy my last few weeks the more without his company. I don't know how he spends his time but in a small town like Funchal there is not much opportunity to get into trouble though I fear he drinks too much.

28 March

Alex and I lunched with the chaplain today. I think Seaton accepted because his father could not come and I expect the colonel left him in safe company with equal relief. Seaton's obsession with Napoleon is well known and has become something of a joke. He did not have to drag it in today as the chaplain kindly introduced the topic into the conversation in all seriousness. Seaton asked to be shown the foundation of the church where Napoleon's louis were buried and the bust of Napoleon, which he insisted on taking down to examine closely. He would have liked to do the same with the Communion Box but this the chaplain refused from motives of reverence. Also he is much more careful about locking everything away since that odd break in. Nothing similar has occurred elsewhere in any part of the island and the chaplain is of the opinion that it was done by a native who saw no sacrilege in breaking into a Protestant church. Recalling the time in the not-too-distant past when all Protestants had to be buried at sea for the Roman church would not allow them to be buried on the island, I suppose the chaplain's theory is as likely as any.

2 April
This will be the last entry in this diary of my stay in Madeira. When I look back to the first pages I realise what I owe to the mild climate and the congenial company I have enjoyed here. My health may not have been totally restored but is certainly much better than it would have been had I returned to the English winter. I can now think of Chitral as just another campaign and accept that, though my army life is over, I can serve the Queen by maintaining my inheritance to the best of my ability.

I paid a last visit to the British Club today. The Aldertons are back in England now and will shortly return to India but as far as one can maintain friendship by correspondence they will remain friends. I could wish that Seaton were more congenial as he is my contemporary but I fear he will never be a friend. I have seen little of him alone in the last week or two and he seems curiously furtive though I know of no specific ill doing which would make me wary of him. Perhaps he too feels that going home on the same ship will give him more than he wants of my company. The colonel will be seeing us off on the ship so I have no need to make a special farewell to him. I bade goodbye to the Gordons when we entertained them to dinner at Reid's. They fulfilled their promise of cuttings and plants and they are already carefully packed and will keep green the memory of my stay in Madeira when transplanted in the garden of the Grange. I hope Macpherson will take a real interest in them. He has occasionally in the past allowed me to insert gifts from my friends in the borders but these will require considerable space and

25

attention and he may still be inclined to treat me as the small boy to whom he allocated a somewhat shady and infertile bit of ground on my eight birthday. However, I go back as master now which will make a difference. Perhaps I should have gone back home last year when both my parents died within a few days of one another but the regiment was constantly on frontier duty and I think my father would have agreed that it would have been cowardice to withdraw from active service. I know now it was the right decision. To have returned to the solitude of the Grange straight after their sudden and unexpected deaths would have been too much. Now I am ready to go to a new life which will be so busy after the estate has been left to subordinates for over a year that I shall be less conscious of the awful gap in my home.

Chapter 5

Gods That Grant Rewards

Rhoda closed the diary with a sigh. If only her father had lived a few years longer so that she could have remembered him as a person instead of a shadowy figure in some very early memories. She realised now where she had acquired her love of solitude. It had certainly not come from her gregarious, much admired mother. She looked out over the sea as her father had done not far off a century before and decided his diary would provide a guide for her activities in Madeira. Hers would be an escapist holiday in this latter-day garden of Eden and, seen from the base of a luxurious hotel, it so proved to be until the intrusion of the serpent.

She liked the impersonal sociability of coach excursions with the fluency of the patriotic guides firmly impressing on tourists the beneficial effects of the Revolution on the inhabitants of the island.

There was a faint reflection of the ethos of Dad's Army, a consoling survival of a time when greed and self interest were not the dominant features of government.

Naturally her first expedition must include the celebrated toboggan ride, not only because it was referred to in her father's diary but she had seen photographs of it and read of travellers from cruise ships bumping down the cobbled slopes in glorious sunshine. This, for one whose experience of foreign climes was limited to visits to France in insular British company, seemed an exotic experience. As she tobogganed down the hill, manoeuvred by the white clad, straw-hatted drivers, she thought of the various legends about how the sport had originated. Was it due to the retired British officer improvising an invalid carriage from a basket chair to get his sick wife to hospital or to the more prosaic need to expedite fresh vegetables to market before the advent of wheeled traffic? Rhoda's companion on this occasion (for a pair was as obligatory on the toboggan as for entry into Noah's Ark) was a dark, intense-looking woman of about thirty. Rhoda recognised her as the woman who, in the church garden on Sunday, had managed to offend even Pixie Putley's large tolerance. How strange that she should have fallen to Rhoda's lot but perhaps not so strange as there seemed to be few singles on the coach and Rhoda had not pressed forward with the first group to reach the slide.

Rhoda noticed her on the coach as a solitary who did not seek to attach herself to anyone else so thought it was safe to exchange names on the brief excursion down the cobbled way. She was pleasantly surprised when her companion included her surname instead of indulging in the pointless familiarity and anonymity of first names only on first acquaintance. Olga Bayne volunteered nothing but her name, though she seemed to want to retain Rhoda's company as they ambled together towards the coach to await the photographic record of their experience.

'I saw a photograph of the toboggan ride as a child.' Olga spoke suddenly, almost involuntarily. 'I've wanted to do it ever since but it should have happened twenty years ago. One outgrows childhood dreams.'

'Not according to Freud. He said happiness was a childhood dream fulfilled in adulthood.'

Olga made no comment.

They both turned to watch the toboggans coming down the slope and Rhoda saw with interest the lorries being loaded, one with the toboggans and the other with the white-clad men. How different from her father's day when little groups came from time to time to arrange with sleighmen individually on a leisurely day's excursion. Now a limited company provided secure jobs for the workers and a brief entertainment for the masses. It was strange to think of holidays as an international industry but they were appreciated by those who could remember a life almost without holidays except in so far as the cessation of work on Sunday could be called a holiday. What will happen when the old generation passes away and the young with their demands for ever more exotic entertainment take over? Even among the old Rhoda heard complaints about the lack of variety on Madeira. Thank goodness they would not reappear on the island but would next year be trying to impress equally blasé friends with cheap souvenirs from Samarkand or the Great Wall of China. Meanwhile her dark companion also seemed lost in meditation.

As they were inevitably combined on the photograph they continued to wait together and Rhoda endeavoured to exchange the few conventional remarks that the situation demanded. Her dark companion had, however, no use for polite conventions. After a glance at the snap she said bitterly, 'I look pretty awful compared with you.' Rhoda had to admit to herself that she did but tried to avoid the point by indicating that her companion was slightly out of focus and, like a passport photograph, it did not do her justice. This was true. Had she done something about the messy tangle of dark hair and substituted an agreeable expression for the dark scowl she habitually wore she would not have been bad looking, in spite of a sallow complexion and eyes of indeterminate shade. Rhoda's well coiffured dark hair and bright blue eyes did invite adverse comparisons with much younger women. Her air of distinction contrasted strongly with Olga's slovenly posture and general air of grievance. Rhoda was reminded of the models on which clothes were now displayed (or at least carelessly hung). To her they looked deformed or depraved – or both.

Desperately Rhoda sought for a way of overcoming her feeling of privileged guilt.

'Would you like to join me for tea at my hotel?'

Olga regarded her suspiciously. Evidently a polite gesture was a sinister move to take advantage of her though how neither she nor anyone else would be able to see.

'All right,' she said finally and, after a pause, 'thank you.'

When they arrived, Rhoda rang room service for tea on the balcony and noticed the black look again on Olga's face. However she responded to Rhoda's courtesies and sat quietly till tea was served.

Rhoda paused with the first cup of tea in hand for her usual contemplation of the sea on the left, the mountains on her right with the curtain of bougainvillea in front of Reid's before her. Olga followed her gaze.

'My view is of the first floor of a warehouse crammed from floor to ceiling with lavatory pans,' she remarked. Rhoda was silenced.

All the amenities of polite society had failed to provide her with a good response to that. She could not prevent herself. She laughed. Surprisingly Olga, instead of commenting bitterly on Rhoda's privileges, smiled grimly herself and said, placatingly,

'I'm scarcely ever in the room in daylight so it doesn't matter but it's a bit of a contrast.'

Rhoda asked how long she was staying in Madeira.

'I don't quite know,' Olga replied. 'A friend of mine is joining me soon and it depends on how he likes it.'

Liberated in general, Rhoda reflected, why do women enslave themselves to a man in particular?

'I was made redundant,' Olga went on. 'Well, may as well tell the truth, I was sacked, so I decided to blow my savings on a good holiday before starting afresh.'

Rhoda waited attentively. Olga must have had few opportunities to talk about herself, for, in spite of Rhoda's obviously cushioned position in life, she overcame her resentment and went on.

'It was one of those dead-end secretarial jobs. You keep the firm going and the boss gets the salary. So I used the computer for a few jobs on the side and he made that excuse for freeing my job for the dolly he'd lined up. I can always get another job like that – I've plenty of experience but it's dead boring.'

Rhoda who had never had to do a salaried job in her life was always at a loss for comment on the world of work and, remembering her disastrous first meeting with Nigel Cooper in Switzerland, wisely held her peace.

After a suitable silence she said,

'So this is your first visit to Madeira? It's mine too. My father came many years before I was born. He kept a diary while he was here.' Her glance went unconsciously to the little brown leather-covered book on her bedside table. 'I thought I should like to visit the places that interested him.'

'I don't know who my father was. I was brought up in an orphanage.'

Rhoda just managed to refrain from gasping. How many of these conversational blockbusters was Olga going to produce? She wished she had tried to get Pixie Putley to join them. In her presence jolly chit-chat was ensured but Constance de Lisle would have resented being left without her companion and at the conjunction of Olga and Constance, to coin a phrase, the mind boggled. Apparently silence was the correct response for Olga went on.

'That's how I came by my name. Even as an infant I was bolshy. I don't dislike it now. I've never met anyone of the same name so that's been a touch of distinction in *my* life.' The humour, though sardonic, seemed genuine and Rhoda had another glimpse of the woman who might have been, had she had a normal childhood.

As if reading her mind Olga said,

'I'd have been very different if I could have got to university.'

'Why not take a degree now?' asked Rhoda. 'There are plenty of opportunities and it would counteract the boredom of your job.'

This was evidently a blockbuster for Olga. She was silent. In her resentment against limited opportunities it had never occurred to her to grasp those that were available. An expression of interest lit up her dark features, then vanished. Some thought had crossed her mind that made this hope illusory. Rhoda guessed it was the man in the background. She thought of the young man who 'went away sorrowful for he had great possessions'. Human beings seemed too often bent on self-destruction, individually and generically.

Six o'clock was approaching and Rhoda saw that Olga was preparing to leave. However inept socially she did not need any form of 'Must you stay? Can't you go?' tactics to speed departure. She even thanked her hostess with some appreciation of her hospitality, and though Rhoda did not suggest another meeting, she felt this one had not been wasted.

As she changed for dinner, she thought regretfully of Matthew Davenport, the friend she had made on her Swiss holiday. It had been a friendship at first sight when they sat together on the plane and then on the coach that had taken them to the guest house where they were booked for the holiday. It was run by two sisters who treated their clients as guests and easy acquaintanceships had developed over after-dinner coffee. The congenial companionship on plane and coach led to Rhoda's missing the trials of single travellers, slow service and awkwardly placed tables in dark corners. Matthew had stayed often at the guest house and invited her to share his privileged position. She enjoyed solitude but there was no doubt that the company of a personable man went for better service and more interesting conversation. She wondered if, after Switzerland, the lesser mountains of Madeira would have any attraction for him.

Tonight, however, there was no need to regret his absence for the first people she saw at the bar were the Grantleys who immediately invited her to join them.

'We usually dine out,' said Mrs Grantley. 'At first it was to entertain Frank's contacts. As they are Portuguese and their wives are sometimes no more fluent in English than I am in Portuguese it was less embarrassing to be in a restaurant with plenty to see and hear than to struggle alone in the apartment while the husbands talked business. I'm not a born cook and having my own job, I never acquired the art sufficiently to enjoy it.'

'What was your job?' asked Rhoda with interest.

'I'm a bricklayer,' replied Mrs Grantley enjoying Rhoda's astonishment.

'She didn't work on building sites,' said Frank handing Rhoda her glass of malmsey.

Harriet laughed. 'It started with art classes. I went to one of those sculpture classes where you used all sorts of materials, wire, wood cast up on beaches, even bricks from building sites. I was no good at producing works of art, with or without good materials and the bricks gave me the idea that I would be better occupied working with them. So the next class I signed up for was bricklaying and I really mastered that and set up my own one-woman business in ornamental walling. I worked mostly in city gardens and was thinking of going on to flint walling when Frank became redundant and we came here.'

Rhoda saw the shadow on Frank's face and hastened to say,

'Why not start up here? Brick walls would be much more attractive than all the cement they have here.'

Harriet was about to reply when Constance de Lisle and Pixie Putley appeared beside them. They recalled having seen the Grantleys in the church garden and Rhoda completed the introductions. Frank turned away to get their drinks and Rhoda breathed a sigh of relief that Harriet's bricklaying was not likely to crop up in conversation again that evening. Pixie had engaged her in conversation while Mrs de Lisle attracted by Frank's pleasant manners accepted her glass of Tio Pepe (no local Madeira for her) and displayed her best side. She ended up asking the Grantleys as well as Rhoda to join them for dinner and this in spite of the fact that Frank had been unable to claim even the most distant relationship with Archdeacon Grantley of Barchester.

As new acquaintances they talked about impersonal things over dinner, their various experiences as tourists providing ample material. Constance and Pixie had visited a museum where they had been impressed by the atmosphere of dignified calm. The unobtrusiveness of the attendants suggested the interest of its treasures rather than their monetary value. Pixie was delighted with the crocodiles of children in red, white and blue overalls, infants with eyes for anywhere but where they were going. At frequent intervals they were telescoped by anxious attendants only to spread incoherently in seconds though each clung to his or her partner's hand throughout. Rhoda too had been attracted by these young scholars and the characters they revealed.

'I watched a toddlers' queue assembling to start a walk. Two tinies had the honour that day of leading the parade. A power struggle was going on behind them for second place. The two given the place by the teacher were very little bigger than the leaders but behind, two much bigger ones were trying to push in front of them. The girl, a potential feminist, edged in but the boy in front was a potential Napoleon. His partner grabbed teacher to bring in adult authority but the boy with boot and elbow was maintaining his position. The status quo was established for half a minute but the struggle began again as a friend of the teacher arrived with a small daughter and they fell into a dramatic conversation. Instantly the feminist pushed forward but evidently only the leaders were allowed to get off the step on to the pavement. For a moment the battle line of four stood on the edge while retreat was cut off by those behind closing up as commanded on their walks. This time the teacher sorted them out with sharp rebukes and all was peace for nearly a minute, like an international cease-fire. After that brief interval of militant tension the battle re-opened. By then the friend's child was attached to the leaders and the queue moved off. I watched them as long as they were in sight and the little feminist continued to attack and the little Napoleon to defend. No prospect of peace was likely until they returned to the classroom where it is to be hoped the combatants were separated widely enough for teacher to give her attention to the law-abiding majority.'

Pixie and the Grantleys smiled appreciatively at Rhoda's effort to fill the long gap between courses. They too had enjoyed watching the crocodiles of tinies and knew enough of children to recognise they were most charming when they were asleep but Mrs de Lisle was more interested in objects than children and genealogical tables more than those whose names figured on them. Moreover, she regarded being kept waiting by waiters as a personal insult and signalled the maître d'hotel to stir up their waiter. This he did in the leisurely manner of the Portuguese and, after a short interval to show they were no longer under a dictatorship, he arrived with a beaming smile to take orders for the next course. While appreciating the comparative cheapness of holidays in Madeira, Mrs de Lisle did not take so kindly to the fact that here the natives regarded the country as their own: tourists benefited from this situation in the absence of theft and crimes of violence common to places where the local population saw the affluence of tourists without sharing in it themselves.

By the time they had retired to comfortable armchairs for coffee it was getting late and the Grantleys, with appreciative comments and requests for the opportunity to return hospitality, set off to their apartment leaving Rhoda to listen to her companions' comments on their new acquaintances.

'Very pleasant people,' said Constance who, a widow, appreciated masculine company and had not heard anything about Harriet's bricklaying activities.

For once, Pixie was able to agree wholeheartedly.

'Do you know what he does?' asked Constance who had a middle-class reticence about asking personal questions but had no intention of remaining in ignorance before allowing the acquaintance to continue.

'Something in finance, I think,' said Rhoda omitting any reference to redundancy and leaving Constance to conjure an image of "merchant banker" which even to her anachronistic vision of society precluded "tradesmen" '.

Pixie added, 'His wife had a job too,' but evidently did not know what it was. This fact diminished the couple's value socially for Constance but to be handed her sherry by a handsome man overrode the handicap of a practical wife. Constance usually found that wives did not come up to the standard of their husbands, unaware that her manner to men was very different from that to women and that they reacted accordingly.

Rhoda wondered whether to throw in Harriet's bricklaying now and see if Constance would contradict her first impressions but decided she liked Pixie too well to spoil her evening, so described

Harriet's job as something to do with landscape gardening. This gave Constance the impression of a hobby made respectable by the interest of the landed gentry in the nineteenth century and, provided they did not make their hands literally dirty, was regarded by Constance as eccentric but not excommunicable.

The mention of gardening naturally led on to planning the inevitable excursion to Blandy's and they arranged to take a taxi there one morning.

'There is an excursion by coach.' Rhoda liked listening to the comments of the local guides and the variety of company encountered on these tours, Constance did not so, not surprisingly, the arrangement about the taxi stood firm. Thinking it over on her return to her room Rhoda decided it was a good thing: Constance's company would preclude any mixing with strangers and a garden needed to be approached at leisure and with due regard to individual interests. Besides, though the Grantleys might be on the excursion, so might Olga, and Rhoda had no intention of exposing her to Constance's snobbery or of cutting her. What an odd mixture the 'civilised' human race was, she thought, as she looked back on the companions of the day. With some surprise she decided that Olga was the most interesting of them all. There was still something to discover about her whereas the others fitted into already known categories.

Chapter 6

The Gates of Paradise

The next day Rhoda decided to have a solitary ramble in the British cemetery. She liked wandering round graveyards at home deciphering old inscriptions and visualising ways of life in the past. She admired the *nihil nisi bonum* which left the sins of the dead to God and their virtues to posterity. The British cemetery attracted her both for this reason and because her father had found it interesting. The Tourist Office was rather vague about its whereabouts but after some discussion managed to indicate the right neighbourhood not far from the English church.

Rhoda wandered slowly up the hill dodging the traffic, parked, and fast moving. What a delightful city Funchal must have been before the advent of the motor car. There were no signs of town planning and no two houses seemed alike. Flowers poured over cement walls and in containers of every sort in courtyards and on stairs and balconies.

She arrived at her destination to find it firmly locked against her behind tall iron gates. 'Odd,' she thought, 'the inhabitants can't get out. Why exclude those who want to get in?' Then she noticed a large bell beside the gate and pressed it rather timidly unwilling to make a din. She waited a while and pressed again more firmly this time and sure she heard the sound of ringing in the distance. She settled down to wait peering through the bars into a walled enclosure. Time passed. When she was sure she had given adequate space for a slow walk, she rang again.

'Keep ringing,' said a lady in English passing by, 'someone will come.'

And someone did come unlocking the great gates and admitting her to the first enclosure. First she just walked along the paths reading the clearest inscriptions and noting that nearly all had died long before the age most people might expect in the affluent West of the current decade. She stopped at the grave of Alexander Stuart of Iridge Place, Sussex and late of Calcutta, who died suddenly on the 16 April. It was a pity to die in the spring. She remembered reading Emily Eden's strictures on the climate of Calcutta. How sad to have escaped only to die in lovely Madeira. She recalled her father's comment on the old-fashioned style of the inscriptions he had read there and saw one dated 1822 but in the classical heroic couplets of the eighteenth century:

> Stranger! These dear remains contained a mind
> As Infants guileless and as Angels kind.
> How good his heart and what his virtues were
> His guardian Angel can alone declare.
> His dearest friend who this poor tribute pays
> Too exquisitely feels to speak his praise.

Here was someone formerly of St Petersburg, late of London; diplomacy or trade? Then a US consul who died at the age of thirty. A lieutenant in the Swedish Navy – what was he doing in Madeira in 1857? A British merchant 'long at Lisbon and late of the Island of Madeira' was notable for length of life. He died at 84 in 1826 and served as a model for ambitious young men:

> By his assiduity and talents he acquired a considerable fortune. He was esteemed by all who knew him for his many social Virtues and amiable Qualities and for soundness of Judgment, perspecuity and energy of mind, honour and integrity he was surpassed by none.

He at least had been given a patriarchal length of life in which to exercise his virtues. A midshipman, aged twenty, an MA of Trinity, Cambridge, a merchant of Liverpool had all been cut off in youth. And here was the eighteen year old, the rolling periods of whose memorial had struck her father sufficiently to copy into his diary.

Here was an even younger victim of nineteenth-century medical ignorance – or heredity, died 1818, aged 15. But what an unusual inscription:

> But Who she was to you reader, is a matter
> of unimportance –
> What she was is the all essential question.

Who had devised these words and what sort of fifteen year old had Sarah been to call forth such an incisive tribute? What would the Constance de Lisles of the world make of it and the contemporary cynics who tell the young, 'It is not what you know but who you know that counts.' Rhoda's speculations turned to the immaculate and anonymous young couple she had sat by on the plane and seen exchanging briefcases in Faro but not a word with anyone. Who or what were they? She had caught a glimpse of the woman once in one of Funchal's more expensive shops but the man she had not seen again and she could not identify a personality in either of them. Olga Bayne, presumably illegitimate and with none of their material advantages, had a positive persona. Perhaps she should have spoken to the couple on the plane but it is difficult to embark on even a conventional remark to people who show no awareness of one's existence even in close physical proximity. What could one write on their tombstones? But they of course would be cremated. Would their ashes be scattered anonymously or was there a golf course, a casino or a racecourse enclosure where they would feel at home? What a lot would be lost to posterity by the absence of tombstones for the present generation. Sarah's could remain unchanged but what about some heroic couplets for the anonymous couple:

> Stranger, these few remains now scattered here
> Are all that's left of two without a peer.
> So shrewd their wits, accounts unnumbered Swiss
> Pay tribute to their fortunes and their bliss.
> No starry-eyed philanthropists were they.
> They lived for money and they took their pay.

Rhoda walked into another enclosure and sat down to watch the lithe brown lizards flashing in and out of the sun-baked grey walls.

The warmth was pleasant and with all these long dead neighbours it behoved her to take a spell of conscious enjoyment of living. Half an hour passed and still the lizards provided signs of life, darting quickly like the butterflies. She rose and decided now to concentrate on the flowers rather than the tombstones. There was every shape and colour and she was not one of those who cared for botanical analysis. As for nomenclature she was of the school who believed a rose by any other name would smell as sweet. Not that she did not appreciate the popular names – bougainvillea had still an exotic sound to her. Frangipani, golden showers, dragon tree all represented 'attar of Stamboul' for her.

She had seen no other pilgrims so doubtless the cemetery guardian was waiting impatiently for her to depart so that he could close the gates. She sauntered to the outer enclosure and saw that after all she was not alone. A woman was seated on the ground evidently sketching details of a plant. Knowing how irritating it was to have people peering over one's shoulder Rhoda walked quickly past and then did a double-take. The artist was familiar. She stopped and turned.

'Martha, Martha Wood,' she exclaimed.

'Rhoda Brown.'

'I enjoyed your Swiss flower book. Are you really preparing one for Madeira?'

Mrs Wood raised herself from the ground and straightened her stiffened limbs.

'Oh, it's good to stretch. Yes, there are magnificent books on Madeiran flowers but a small lightweight one for easy identification that can be put in a handbag should prove profitable, so here I am for the next few weeks.'

'I must not interrupt you now,' said Rhoda and Mrs Wood was too straightforward to pretend it would be convenient to stop work.

'Have you been to Blandy's yet?' she asked. 'I want to spend a morning doing a preliminary survey to decide what to include from the great gardens and we could go round together.'

'That would be delightful. I had planned to go this week with two acquaintances from my hotel. Would you prefer I came with you alone?'

'Oh no. The book is intended for the tourist market so it will be helpful to find out what flowers they are interested in and how much information they want to absorb.'

'Well, you couldn't have two more different people to hear from. Mrs Constance de Lisle is on one extreme of snobbish detachment and Miss Pixie Putley at the other for interest in everything especially her fellow men and women.'

'I shall look forward to meeting them.'

Rhoda rightly took this as an indication that Martha wanted to get back to work so stayed only to exchange telephone numbers and addresses, promising to ring up after consulting the others as to a convenient morning. She then made her way down towards the sea front stopping en route for a cup of coffee at one of the cafés in the meagre pedestrian precinct in the city centre.

The coffee was welcome but even more agreeable was the freedom from traffic and the mixture of local people, tourists and passengers from the cruise ship currently in the harbour, in the cafés and wandering by. Rhoda suddenly became aware of a small Artful Dodger motionless beside her. She turned to see the deliberately mournful eyes of a small boy. He presented a shoe box with a slit in the top. Rhoda turned away but it was too late. She had met his eyes and was thereby compelled to fish out a couple of small coins and insert them in the box. The Artful Dodger, well aware of their infinitesimal value, stood his ground but retreated in good order as she snapped her purse shut. How civilised Madeira is. In Avignon three such angelic creatures had skilfully removed her purse and vanished into limbo before she aware of her loss.

Joining Constance and Pixie for lunch, she suggested the addition of Martha Wood to their expedition to Blandy's. They were pleased to have a fourth to fill the taxi and agreed to leave it to Rhoda to arrange for any morning Mrs Wood cared to name. Rhoda told them what she knew of Martha, a Battle-of-Britain widow left with a son , Chester, to bring up, who had taken to a prosperous career in oil. Martha had discovered a talent of her own for flower painting and now had several successful books to her name.

'I think I have one,' said Constance unexpectedly. 'Woodland Flowers of Romania. It was a prize at the annual village bridge drive. I was partner to Lady Mary Bedford you remember Pixie.'

Pixie had good cause to remember as Constance's friends were not likely to forget the occasion, being reminded of it whenever the subject of bridge came up.

'A very attractive book,' she said good-naturedly, 'it will be a pleasure to meet the artist.'

'A very odd prize though,' said Constance. 'No one there had ever been to Romania or was likely to go. Probably a cheap remainder,' she added tactlessly. 'I wasn't on the prize committee that year and Mrs Kingstone (the rector's wife you know) does not believe in good prizes. She thinks the extra money should all go to the cause and people should be satisfied with the game.'

'Quite right,' said Pixie stoutly. 'At my old school we had in the prayers every Friday, "May we love the game more than the winning or the prize", and that was supposed to get us in the right mood for Saturday matches.'

'And did it?' asked Rhoda, who had probably been the last girl outside the royal family to be educated by a governess and so knew nothing of team spirit.

'Oh, I think so. What you don't expect you don't miss.'

'Well I expect suitable prizes at a bridge drive. It adds to the interest and is a stimulus for bringing good partners. There were people chatting during the game at the last village drive. Whatever the prayers, I'm sure you took your games seriously, Pixie.'

'Yes, but then we were under severe discipline and sent off the field if we chatted so we hadn't much chance to be frivolous, whereas the village drives are intended to be social occasions.'

'Do you play bridge, Miss Brown?'

Mrs de Lisle obviously expected the answer yes. Rhoda found her mind wandering to Latin grammar and wondered if *pons* would do for 'bridge' though she had forgotten that the particles varied according to the affirmative or negative answer. Then, realising Constance was puzzled by the pause, said firmly,

'No. My mother was very keen to the end of her life so I made it my business to entertain the non-players at her drives.' Rhoda felt a little dishonest at this reply though it was a partial truth but she did not think it necessary to confess she loathed the game and found it distasteful even to watch the devotees.

'Very proper,' said Constance but Rhoda caught a sharp glance from Pixie and knew she guessed what Rhoda's true opinion was.

Rhoda realised that Pixie was much more quick witted than her air of good-natured benevolence suggested and remembered a politician's remark that it was always better to appear somewhat less intelligent than one really was. There was, too, the biblical theme that a name was a power and knowledge of it gave power over the owner. Pixie was not an abbreviation, but the actual name

41

given the unfortunate child by a silly little mother. As Pixie had clearly taken after her father in size and intelligence, Rhoda guessed that the simple, straightforward mask she presented to the world concealed a shrewd judge of character and a way of coping with the stupidities of friends like Constance whose masks seemed the only character they had.

They separated after lunch and Rhoda decided to go for a walk in the nearby gardens where country and sea views could be equally enjoyed. As she reached the entrance she stood to watch a kindergarten cross the road, boys and girls alike protected by pinafores that recalled Victorian nurseries in the illustrations of Mrs Molesworth's books. When she moved to Half Acre, Rhoda had taken with her a complete edition of these works which had belonged to her mother and had read a number of them with admiration of the knowledge of child psychology acquired through observation by the best Victorian writers for children. They therefore presented whole personalities instead of the results of clinical analysis which produced the cardboard silhouettes of so much contemporary writing. Their mental age was no doubt far in advance of the Carrots and Hermy and This and That of Mrs Molesworth's novels but they enjoyed little of the childhood reflected there and, having missed it, reverted to its irresponsibilities in adult life. Olga Bayne must be about thirty but, she reflected, with the moods and 'cut off your nose to spite your face' mentality of adolescence.

Rhoda realised she was not looking at the scene she had come to see and, seating herself near some harsh-fronded palms, she gave herself up to immediate enjoyment. The sun shone clearly, the sea was azure, to use a favourite epithet of Shelley and the atmosphere that which must have inspired Browning's famous evocation of the occasional fleeting moments of perfect happiness:

> God's in his heaven
> All's right with the world.

Sociable groups of gardeners were working and chatting in convivial bands of four. What if they chatted more than they worked? It was surely better than in the 'advanced' societies where management raced in maniacal pursuit of wealth and workers in resentful boredom and yet 'work' was regarded as an essential to self respect and to be 'unemployed' was a moral blemish. Rhoda woke to the

42

fact that the presence of human beings tended to lead to bitter reflections and got up to find a seat where she could look over them to the sea.

Madeira was ideal for escapism and Rhoda returned refreshed to the hotel to embark on her daily swim in the comfort of a heated pool and when most people had left the pool side as shadow crept over the area. It was the time of day when few were in the pool and she could follow her routine of adding a length to the target of the previous day without having to dodge the splashing crawls of the men or the displaying dives of the women.

By the time she was in her room and dressed for dinner, she thought Martha Wood would be back in her apartment and rang up to complete arrangements for the visit to Blandy's garden the next day. Martha was there to answer the phone and was ready for a new area of subjects having finished a long day at the British cemetery.

Next day, having found a taxi driver with a moderate supply of English, they all set off for Blandy's. Constance made no effort to find out whether Martha belonged to any particular Woods. Even to her a Battle-of-Britain husband was superior to anyone to be found in Debrett's. For Pixie it was sufficient to find someone who could share her love of nature, not herself being interested in genealogy. The short drive to Blandy's was enlivened by the taxi driver who pointed out features of interest en route, the inclusion of 'Ishbishcus' providing an attractive introduction to the most characteristic sound in Portuguese. So interesting did they find his commentary that they asked him to return at the end of the morning, a good taxi driver being able to make the difference between agreeable or exasperating excursions.

As they had arrived earlier than the main excursionists, their first sight of the house and garden was unimpeded by others and Martha's preoccupation with her notebook involved the others in a very leisurely pace. But everywhere they paused there was something lovely to look at. Of course many gardens in England were equally lovely but the balmy atmosphere guaranteed in Madeira was missing there. Rhoda remembered many occasions standing in a bitter east wind or sometimes even a scorching sun to admire some new addition a proud owner wanted to show off. Here one could sit in comfort while others pursued detailed examinations of shape and category while she enjoyed colour and atmosphere.

The garden was beginning to fill as groups of tourists arrived on conducted tours. Rhoda thought she caught a glimpse of Olga Bayne in the distance but she was not coming in their direction though Rhoda was interested to see that a young man seemed to be accompanying her. Rhoda would have sauntered their way as she was curious to know what sort of young man could have so strong an influence but possibly he was just another of the tour and, on his own, had drifted along with the only unattached female. Rhoda herself had acquired companions of varied nationalities in these circumstances and found that men were often more reluctant than women to walk alone. Meanwhile, Olga, if it were she, had gone out of sight and Rhoda's companions were moving off in the opposite direction.

They were now in the area where the crumbling mansion of the original owner stood. Rhoda wondered how many old Portuguese families had died out or been compelled by financial reasons to part with estates to English Madeirans. But for the Napoleonic wars would there be many English there in spite of the long-standing alliance? Charles II had certainly missed a chance to acquire by marriage a beautiful island but would it have the same quality if it had become part of the British Empire? Suppose Napoleon had taken it?

Rhoda suddenly noticed an expensive young man examining the building and wondered why he looked familiar. He was one of the anonymous pair of her plane journey. He was clutching a brief-case and seemed the last person to be interested in getting his hands dirty gardening. Perhaps it was architecture that had brought him here with a view to some fantastic development accessible only to those in the over-a-million house-price range? He too disap-peared while Martha and Pixie had their heads together over a rare lily, the commoner Arum being attraction enough for Rhoda whose father had donated the Easter lilies annually to the parish church.

The morning passed as quickly and more peaceably than one at Chelsea Flower Show and now they were proceeding up the Camellia Avenue strewn with fallen blossoms like the path to the church after a Victorian village wedding.

Their taxi driver awaited them at the entrance and Rhoda took the precaution of getting his name and telephone number, English-speaking taxi drivers not being as plentiful as one might expect, though one had to remember how recent the Portuguese Revolution was with concomitant benefits like an adequate educational system. They stopped for a drink together before Martha returned to her flat to organise her morning's notes.

While Rhoda went to the bar to collect drinks, the others perched on a bench, Constance looking her haughtiest to counteract the undignified position in which she found herself. She had some time to wait as the barman not only served the locals first but betrayed the old-fashioned contempt for single women and attempted to leave her till last. However, a Scandinavian firmly said, 'This lady was first,' pushing himself in front of a man of another nationality who shared the local prejudice. As the Scandinavian was almost twice the size of the pushing tourist, Rhoda secured the drinks for her party from the reluctant barman and, thanking her companion, joined the hen party on the perch.

Mrs de Lisle sipped her sherry reluctantly as, though the glass had been washed it had not been dried and polished, while the others without regard for the container, were blowing their heads off with local poncha, which Martha said was the most stimulating beverage she'd ever met in all her travels. But one was enough for them to depart in high good humour and a slight uncertainty of gait which made Rhoda glad they had a taxi waiting and Constance to accompany them with increased hauteur.

Rhoda knew she was going to regret that glass of poncha. She had suggested it only because she had become irritated with Constance's eternal, 'A dry sherry – *very* dry.' She didn't really care for alcohol as the dominant ingredient in a drink and, besides a slight dizziness, she had the beginnings of a headache. She had time to get irritated with the careful negotiations over the exact proportion of the taxi fare for each, as Martha was taking it on to her outlying flat, and made the mistake of trying to pay the whole fare herself which offended everyone, especially as she gave the driver a handsome tip on her own behalf.

'It arouses false expectations to do that,' said Constance, 'and the drivers then raise the fares for tourists.'

For a moment Rhoda felt some sympathy with an ill-bred youth who once told Mrs de Lisle to 'Drop dead' when she tackled him for dropping litter but stopped herself in time by saying,

'I have enjoyed our morning. Thank you for your company,' and, waving to Martha, made for the first available lift and got to her room to put her feet up and order lunch in her own room.

45

'For *one*?' came the inevitable query as she phoned her order – as if one's own company would destroy anyone's appetite.

'For *one*,' she replied briskly putting the phone down.

An hour's sleep after lunch restored her equanimity but she decided she had had enough company for the day and would go to tea at the former British Club on her own. Here the smiling students raised her spirits and a comfortable basket chair on the terrace in the sun brought her father's diary to mind. The greater part of a century had passed since he had been here before her and the thought of the passage of time made her remorseful at losing her sense of proportion. The tall tree in front of her, only a few years old when her long-dead father had seen it, brought home the fleeting nature of human life.

The British Club where Captain Brown had consumed Scotch and soda, or would it have been gin and tonic? with Colonel Seaton was a rendezvous with her father's memory that Rhoda had wished to make. Now named the Quinta Magnolia and, free to the public, it had lost its exclusive grandeur but none the less served the social purpose of the old club. Rhoda was approached by two couples asking to join her as the terrace was filling up. They turned out to be total contrasts as hotelmade friends often are, having been thrown together by propinquity to establish an attraction of opposites. One couple was Manchester born and bred, blunt of speech and betraying a sense of humour; the others were as obviously from the south and so conventional in outlook as to serve as a foil for the others. Rhoda was reminded during their conversation of cross-talk comedians, the southerners providing remarks from which the northerners struck off repartee, with no little wit. For once she was glad to have her chosen solitude broken into. However, she had long finished her tea, so having paid her bill she said goodbye to her companions with gratitude for the detachment with which they replied, neither showing pleasure at getting rid of a single person nor pity at her being alone.

Rhoda wanted to get closer to the curtain of rose-coloured bougainvillea that draped a wall on the opposite side of the garden and found it well worth inspection. The close view from the terrace was probably as attractive as in her father's day but the distant scene was cut off by a flat line of buildings not high rise but of sufficient height to block out the inland hills. As the way back to her hotel was downhill she decided to walk back by which time the last fumes of poncha would have evaporated.

It seemed now accepted that she would dine with Pixie and Constance and they had grown sufficiently familiar with one another for the occasional silence to present no strain. Since they had separated at the end of the morning they had sufficient material for conversation in exchanging news of their activities.

Constance was prepared to forget the somewhat unladylike effect of the poncha in return for Rhoda's father having been a member of the former British Club.

'What sort of people go there now?' she asked.

'It's open to the public but it was mostly tourists who were having tea on the terrace. I was joined by two couples representing the north/south divide and found them very good company.'

'We've been down to the Beatles' boat,' said Pixie, averting Constance's inevitable comment on the unintelligibility of the northern accent. 'It's now a restaurant. The name attracts tourists.' She ignored Constance's snort and went on, 'It's a very pleasant spot for a warm afternoon. We were going to ring your room to see if you would like to join us but thought you might be tired after our long morning,' tactfully refraining from referring to the visible effects of poncha.

Rhoda wondered how Pixie would cope with Olga Bayne as a guest for dinner. If someone as acceptable to Constance as she was required all this alertness to avoid social disturbance, Pixie's life must be one long watch for pitfalls. She thought Constance's friendship was scarcely worth it but guessed that Pixie would always be loyal to childhood friends and knew how these arose among people of opposite interests and temperament. She said good night early and Constance watched her speculatively as she went towards the lift.

'Do you think she drinks?' she asked Pixie.

'Nonsense, of course she doesn't,' replied Pixie with unusual brusqueness. 'You really should not say things like that. Gossip can spread round a hotel as quickly as in a village and you don't know where it will end.'

'Yes, but she did seem a bit tiddly after that poncha.'

'If she drank she wouldn't show the effects after one poncha. It's just it's very strong. Mrs Wood and I were both a little dizzy when

47

we first got up from the bench. She's obviously *less* used to strong drink than we are.'

'Well, I'll stick to sherry,' said Constance unusually pacifically, for Pixie seemed really annoyed for once.

'Yes, *very* dry.' There was a rare touch of malice in Pixie's voice but even she was sometimes irritated by the implication that there was something superior in a taste for dry sherry rather than sweet Madeira.

If Constance noticed it she ignored the tone and resolved the situation by waving to a couple of acquaintances to join them. The husband was in a 'superior' branch of the civil service (not Social Services of course) so they were quite acceptable as companions for drinks especially as the wife too liked sherry '*very* dry'.

Chapter 7

The Golden Journey

Next morning Rhoda, having as usual enjoyed coffee and rolls in the solitude of her own room, strolled down to the swimming pool. It was too early for it to be crowded and the children's pool had only one occupant, who however was taking up a good deal of space. A small girl, she was processing round the pool pulling a train of inflated objects behind her. Rhoda stopped to watch her and immediately two identical little boys appeared, regarding her suspiciously.

'We're looking after her,' one said, 'she's our sister.'

'Oh,' said Rhoda, 'she's a great responsibility no doubt.'

'She's the Princess of Wales getting married,' said the other twin.

'Hullo,' said Rhoda tentatively to the abstracted child.

'You can speak to her if you like,' said one brother to the little girl. She showed no inclination to take advantage of the privilege but proceeded unmoved round the pool.

'Where is the Prince?' asked Rhoda.

The child stopped, looked affectionately at her train (which indeed looked in its crumpled masses not unlike the real original) and solemnly considered the question. After looking speculatively at her brothers,

'He's gone to the loo. I can't wee in this dress.'

'I suppose not,' said Rhoda, pondering the problem of nervous royalty. She turned to the boys. Either they had recognised her as part of Sunday's congregation or she had passed muster as a desirable character for they had gone back to their own activities. The

49

Princess too had resumed processing leaving Rhoda feeling superfluous and at a loss as she often felt with young children.

Fortunately at that moment Mrs Roscommon appeared and, joining Rhoda, fell easily into conversation after the manner of clerical wives.

'I'm Olivia Roscommon. I saw you in church on Sunday.'

'Yes, I recognised the children. I'm Rhoda Brown.'

The little girl was looking to her mother for admiration or participation.

'Come along Your Highness. You've been in the pool long enough. Mark, John, come along and deflate Bea's train. The attendant is very good keeping an eye on them when Barnabas and I have to be away together. He wanted me to come with him to visit a woman in one of the Time Share flats – her husband died suddenly of a heart attack.'

'Would you like to come up to my room for coffee? Visits like that take it out of you. The children can use the bathroom there. I've got a family room for my single room supplement.'

'Thank you,' said Mrs Roscommon, without demur, 'that will be very pleasant.'

Mark and John had meanwhile disentangled the princess from her train, deflated the component parts and stuffed them in a plastic bag leaving Bea to hurl herself on her mother in a wet bathing costume. Olivia gave her a hug and the boys a thank you with a friendly slap and they went up with Rhoda to her room.

'Just turn them loose in the bathroom. They'll be all right,' said Olivia handing another plastic bag to one of the boys. She and Rhoda sat down in comfortable armchairs and Rhoda rang room service for coffee and ice creams.

'How long have you been in Madeira?'

'Nearly six months. We are here for a year by which time we hope Barnabas will be fully recovered. What the next job will be we don't know. The man who's taken over Barny's parish is getting on very well so will probably stay now for three or four years. I'd like a university chaplaincy where good schools would be handy for the children but Barnabas might think it a soft option in which case we'll be back to inner city.'

'You might have both; university towns have their losers' areas now.'

'That's true. Anyway I find it best to live in the present. The world always seems to be on the verge of some catastrophe or other so it's best to get on with whatever comes to hand.'

What came to hand at that moment were the three children. Beatrice now in dry pants and the boys with moderately clean hands and hair well brushed.

'How very capable they are.'

'Yes, I believe children should be as independent as possible and should spend their time as far as possible with other children, not subjected before their time to the strains of adult life. That's why I was pleased that you put them on the balcony with their ice creams where their own chatter will prevent them from hearing what we say.'

Rhoda was rather surprised at the outspoken way in which Olivia talked about their family life on a first meeting but came to realise that as long as she spoke out there was less room for lying gossip from which all public personalities and, most of all, clergy of the Church of England suffer. Also she could imagine the sort of interviews in an inner-city rectory from which parents would want children excluded and to do this without neglect needed careful planning and training.

The telephone rang and Rhoda lifted the receiver.

'Barnabas Roscommon here. They tell me at the desk you have my family with you, Miss Brown.'

'Will you join us?'

'Thank you. I'll come straight up.'

Rhoda rang for fresh coffee, first checking with Olivia that decaffeinated was not required. Coffee and the rector arrived together so Barnabas evidently had not managed to come straight up. As he wore his clerical collar Rhoda was not surprised. Without belonging to any church, most people assumed that a clergyman had nothing to do except on Sunday so was free to listen to their troubles, questions or attacks at any time on any other day.

He greeted Rhoda, smiled at his wife and went straight out on to the balcony to get a boisterous greeting from the children. He left them to 'I Spy', Beatrice being allowed to win once in three, regardless of what her guess began with as her knowledge of the alphabet was partial and uncertain.

'Is Mrs Field better?' asked Olivia, assuming correctly that Rhoda was interested in the rector's activities.

'Yes, I found the couple she knows at their hotel and fortunately they are nearly at the end of their holiday so they will be able to accompany her on the flight home. The courier is assuming all the business about getting the coffin back and there are two grown-up daughters so there's adequate support back home if any support is adequate in bereavement.'

Rhoda handed him his coffee and she and Olivia embarked on second cups, changing the conversation to Rhoda's interests so that Barnabas could have his in peace. Rhoda started a gentle monologue about her activities in Madeira and how she had come to visit the island while the others sank back in their armchairs and relaxed.

When a spat arose between Mark and John, Olivia called the children in and suggested they should all go back to the swimming pool, inviting Rhoda to join them. She decided it would be better for them to have a family party and, thanking them for visiting her, said she was going out shortly. Bea, having returned to her princess role at the mention of the swimming pool, offered her hand to Rhoda to kiss, Rhoda luckily guessing the significance of the gesture and refraining from putting a chocolate in the outstretched hand. The boys pushed Bea on and Rhoda shook hands with the parents hearing that free use of the swimming pool for the whole family was a perk granted by the hotel manager in return for the promptitude with which the rector responded when called on behalf of any of the hotel guests.

'It's a real boon,' said Olivia, 'as the Portuguese are so good with children. We can leave them happily under the eye of the pool attendant if we are called out together at this end of the town.'

Rhoda told them of the prompt attention of the boys when she first paused by the children's pool and they laughed but said they insisted on the three sticking together in their own parish even when inside the rectory yard which, though part of a tight housing estate, provided a wall against which ball games could be played. This provided occupation both for their own children and those of people coming to the rectory for help and having no one to leave them with in their own homes.

'It means our kids have to be gregarious and learn to get on with anyone in the neighbourhood and they don't notice whether they are black or white, Jew or Gentile. Good training for the twenty-first century,' said Barnabas with the first sign of political irony that Rhoda had observed in him.

The gregarious three were showing signs of restiveness, Beatrice aiming kicks at her brothers' shins which they had become adept at avoiding, especially as she tried to get both at the same time. Having been told that, as they were bigger they were not to hit her, they were dodging round the balcony furniture at a high speed which was becoming dangerous. Barnabas called them in and Rhoda was pleased to see they grasped their parents' hands but did not indulge in tale-telling. John remembered the long-ago consumed ice cream and thanked Rhoda, the others joining in belatedly. They departed leaving Rhoda thinking how easily the morning had gone with no underlying conflicts to smooth over or ignore.

As she had booked a *levada* walk for the next morning she decided a swim and a walk in the park would be sufficient exercise for the day. She should have time for correspondence – the inevitable flood of postcards to acquaintances and letters for Matthew Davenport, the friend made on her Swiss holiday, and for the Mackenzies, the couple who maintained Half Acre, Mackenzie as an extension of his market garden and his wife as a change from cooking for the Vice-Chancellor of Stoneborough University who inhabited the Grange, formerly the home of Rhoda's family.

Late in the afternoon she went to the park, where she was approached by a small beggar offering a flower head obviously just picked from an adjacent bed. She shook her head and he left with a charming grin which Rhoda involuntarily returned. Even the beggars here were neither drunk nor aggressive. She surmounted the problem of finding a seat in the sun free of courting couples by perching on a stone wall, to the dismay of the lizards who had been sunning themselves there. A three-masted sailing ship lay at anchor in the harbour. Strange how the beauty of inanimate objects seemed to be in inverse proportion to the comfort of human beings associated with them. Rhoda remembered a TV programme in which the commentator described life on one of these beautiful vessels. The sailors dried off their storm-soaked clothes by sleeping in them. She recalled watching a young man negotiating the frail scaffolding round the cathedral and wondering how many injuries and deaths had gone into the creation of these lovely buildings and how many lives were shortened by services in the piercing cold within them. It was pleasanter to watch the black swans in the pond, their feathers ruffled by the breeze.

A family passed with its complement of jolly little dark-eyed bambinos. An elderly couple came along, the man suffering from the cruel trouser fashion accentuating overhanging bellies. Now came a young couple and Rhoda started. The woman was Olga Bayne and with her presumably the young man who had such a strong influence over her. Rhoda said, 'Good afternoon' and Olga started in her turn. She obviously did not wish to introduce the young man but he had easier manners than she and commented on the view and the skill of the wind surfers. He was quite attractive though probably some years younger than Olga whose resentful expression prevented Rhoda from trying to extend the conversation.

'Come *on* Alec: we'll be late.' Though it was clear the young man did not know for what they would be late he took his leave gracefully and with Olga's muttered goodbye they departed. Rhoda wondered how on earth they had come together. Though good looking and with surface charm, he did not convey strength of character. Possibly the association had begun over Olga's computer sidelines. Her dismissal suggested they had not been exactly above board. Olga had not seemed to want them to meet. Perhaps she regretted her confidence in Rhoda. She was also intelligent enough to know that any observer might be struck by the difference of ages and surface attraction between them and wonder what he saw in her. With Rhoda it was the reverse. What could Olga see in him? He could be duplicated in any bar while she was really unusual.

Rhoda gave up meditating on the contradictions of human nature and returned to watching the wind surfers while the cruise ship in the harbour belched the smoke of affluent civilisation over the bay. Some time remained before dinner so she decided to go into the town and have her hair done. Hotel hairdressers had a sameness in style and expense; the local ones had more individuality and were certainly cheaper. They seemed amused by tourists which gave the tourist the pleasureable feeling of entertaining rather than adding to a heavy work load. In Madeira the visitor could be another person not just an additional statistic in the tourist industry.

Rhoda joined Constance and Pixie for dinner looking her best. Having played second fiddle to her mother all her life, she was not aware of glances of involuntary admiration as she passed. She enjoyed shopping at the Stoneborough boutique, which had caught her distinctive style and always had something special for her when she went away but hers was not the generation given to personal remarks, so she took the commendations of the assistants as professional courtesies. But Pixie was conscious of an unusual feeling of envy as the stylish figure approached and even Constance, who had always an expensive outfit for any occasion, realised she did not achieve Rhoda's air of distinction. It did not disturb Mrs de Lisle's self-satisfaction but had they lived in the same circle, Rhoda would have found herself the target of derogatory remarks.

Rhoda ordered a sweet Madeira and decided she must refrain from saying, '*Very* sweet' even mentally lest she should one day say it aloud in Constance's presence. Conversation was sluggish at first as all had spent a lazy afternoon but interest quickened when they found Rhoda had spent the morning with the Roscommon family. Pixie was genuinely interested in the haggard cleric who acted on his belief that Christianity was for the poor and oppressed and Constance was intrigued that a Roscommon of Tayside should jettison the privileges of birth and fortune.

'Estimable but decidedly odd.' She could admire but not approve.

Pixie was more interested in the children who followed their father in being 'all things to all men' and were therefore more agreeable company for visitors than most children.

'They seem to get on extraordinarily well together,' said Rhoda.

'That's because they are treated as persons not appendages.' Pixie really was very perceptive under that jolly façade.

As Constance was not interested in children they were not attracted to her so she turned the conversation to the next day's activities.

'If the weather holds, I think we should have tea at Reid's. We need a still day as it can be chilly on the terrace. It is amusing watching the tourists. They don't allow parties but all the tours encourage people to go.'

It never occurred to Constance that she was a tourist. To her tourists were those who travelled in coaches instead of taxis and were not averse to showing their enjoyment when on holiday.

Rhoda would have liked to make her first visit on her own but the others had suggested it and it would be awkward if she turned up alone on a day they chose to go.

'I'm going on a guided *levada* walk in the morning so it will be pleasant to have a restful afternoon. My father stayed at Reid's when he was here on his way back from India and he commented on the view from the terrace in his diary.'

'Good, that's a definite engagement then. We'll meet you in the lobby at a quarter to four and walk up. It's not worth taking a taxi for such a short distance.'

Constance opened her mouth to dissent on this point but Rhoda had noticed she often refrained from bringing on herself Pixie's blunt comments on snobbery. Instead she turned to Rhoda.

'You seem to like mixed company,' she said on a note of incredulity.

'I do,' replied Rhoda firmly. 'You meet people whom you would never see otherwise.'

'That's what I object to.'

Pixie met Rhoda's eye but neither made any comment leaving even Constance with a feeling of having been less than tactful. Rhoda left them together as she wanted an early night with a view to an energetic morning ahead.

Chapter 8

The Strangest of Adventures

'How can I describe the fascinations of a walk along the *levada:?*' Like her father, Rhoda had got hold of Ellen Taylor's description of her visit to Madeira in 1882 and had been impressed by how little of the island's charm had suffered from the influx of tourists a century later. No one can describe the fascinations of an experience which has no appeal or no parallel for some one else. If walking were associated with sore feet or the absence of a 'prestigious' car or the boredom of being in the country out of sight or sound of bars and discos, there was nothing fascinating about a *levada* walk. But Rhoda loved the remoteness from the crowds and traffic of Funchal and found the other *levada* walkers did too.

A small flotilla of taxis had carried about twenty people to the beginning of the walk. Rhoda had hoped that Martha Wood would be one of them but her congenial company was given sparingly. She probably went alone along the *levadas* in her pursuit of subjects for her tourists' guide to Madeira's flowers, though she might have gained advice for her selection from enthusiastic walkers. Instead Rhoda was surprised and not especially pleased to see Olga Bayne emerge from one of the taxis but, after a casual greeting, she showed no sign of wishing to attach herself to Rhoda. She was alone and presumably did not wish to explain Alec's absence.

The column of all ages and various nationalities straggled along, sometimes exchanging remarks, more often just ambling, shuffling through the fallen leaves or striding out of sight of those stopping to look downwards at a view through the trees or to enjoy the sight, here growing freely in the wild, of flowers that had to be coaxed through life in northern Europe.

After Switzerland, Rhoda might have found it monotonous to go so long on a level path but, though one had to keep an eye open for projecting stones and tree roots, the pleasure of steady movement and the sound of running water were variety enough for those who could create their own amusements and to whom the speed which enabled people to save a few minutes on a car journey was anathema. Rhoda often wondered, when she heard the boasting of doing a journey in five minutes less than another driver, what marvel of experience the 'saved' five minutes was destined for to make it worth while. But 'save' had become a magic formula in advertising resulting in the opposite connotation from its use in Rhoda's childhood. 'Spend three hundred pounds on a washing machine, thereby "saving" twenty-five pounds.' No wonder words were becoming empty of meaning. What an array of historical footnotes and linguistic analysis would be required in the present decade to communicate the meaning of St John's term for the central truth of Christianity.

Rhoda's train of thought was interrupted by her awareness that a man was walking beside her. He had evidently recognised her and, after a moment, she realised he was one member of the northern couple she had met at the Quinta Magnolia. She looked round.

'Isn't your wife with you?'

'No. She was a nurse before we married and now her feet won't stand up to long walks. She likes lounging by the swimming pool and the Wintons didn't want to come so she has company.'

Rhoda assumed the Wintons to be the conventional southern couple who had been with them at the club and was not surprised that wandering in the remote countryside had no appeal for them.

'What attracts you to these walks?' she asked.

'Well I jog at home and I don't find just swimming provides enough exercise. I'm a bit of a naturalist too.'

This proved an over-modest statement as he was able to name clearly all the plants and trees they passed.

'I miss the birds though. We'd have seen a dozen different species by now in a walk at home.'

'My father felt that too. He visited Madeira many years ago and

58

commented on the lack of birds in his diary. He hadn't much interest in sea birds and there aren't many others here.'

'They say it's because the island isn't on a migration route, but I wonder if it isn't due to hunters shooting them. Any moving target seems fair game to some of them especially on the continent.'

A young Dutchman overheard that and came up to join in the conversation and Rhoda dropped back to a slower pace. She wanted to absorb her surroundings not discuss them and to enjoy the scent and sound of the pines.

> For pines are gossip pines the wide world through
> And full of runic tales to sign and sing.

Whatever the shortcomings of her governess education Rhoda was grateful for the foundation of a lifelong habit of absorbing poetry by heart so that she had a fund of expression for her perceptions. For a mile she walked alone, the others out of sight round turns in the path either ahead or behind her. They closed up as they came to a waterfall, the photographers among the fast walkers bringing them to a standstill enabling the guide, sheepdogging in the rear to get her flock together again.

Olga Bayne came up with the rear group and joined Rhoda.

'Quite beautiful, isn't it?' she said amiably referring to the waterfall.

'Yes, and partly because it's small and therefore quiet. Thundering waterfalls are too much of a good thing. It's one of the things I like about Madeira. The mountains are not too high, the trees are not too large.'

'The people are not too tall,' Olga interrupted humorously for her. 'Alec finds it all rather small beer. He has travelled the world and has big ideas.'

'Doesn't he care for *levada* walks?'

'No, he's not the athletic type. He's looking for some temporary work to raise a bit of cash. He's always worked his way on his travels. He plays his guitar and sings if nothing else crops up.'

Rhoda suspected this to be his chief occupation. He had looked too easy going to be fond of hard work and the travelling musician seemed now to be replacing the eternal student. Rhoda had friends at home who objected to the revival of street musicians but Rhoda rather liked them provided they did not use amplifiers.

59

'Street musicians usually look young and cheerful and, if they hitchhike they don't add to the number of cars choking narrow old city streets. Not every young man is able to follow a profession and lead a life of cut-throat competition. I don't sit lightly to possessions myself having a good inheritance but I admire those who can abandon them altogether and take life as it comes.'

'It's all right when you're young,' said Olga reverting to her natural gloom, 'but it's no fun when you get older.'

'Even the old tramps sitting on park benches, bottle in hand, seem to enjoy life more than the harassed young executives that crowd commuter trains.'

Olga scowled. The orphanage upbringing had indoctrinated the Pauline attitude, 'He who does not work, neither shall he eat,' and Rhoda's light-hearted comments aroused the '*You* don't know what it's like' response from her. Rhoda was rather ashamed of having been betrayed by Olga's unwonted good humour into speaking without thinking. It was true she did not know what Olga's life was like. It was so far from her sphere of experience that she could not imagine being alone and poor. Perhaps even Alec was a good influence for her in sharing her situation but not allowing it to immerse him in gloom.

Rhoda tried to think of something conciliatory to change the subject but Olga in a black mood was inhibiting. However, at that point the photographers having finished, set off again at a brisk pace up a few steps in a rise in the path. Rhoda followed in relief leaving Olga behind. Whether she slipped or really felt a slight push she could never afterwards be sure but she fell, striking her leg hard against one of the steps which had a sharp edge. The pain made her feel faint for a moment and she sat down on one of the steps with her head in her hands. Olga was nearest and immediately got some first aid equipment out of her bag. She rolled up the trouser leg revealing a nasty gash and very efficiently cleaned it and put some ointment and a dressing on the wound. As the width of the steps allowed for only one person at a time, those in front walked on slowly and the others held back out of the way. Olga obviously knew what to do and got on with it. Only the guide kept a careful eye on the proceedings.

Rhoda got up saying, 'It's nothing. I can carry on quite well,' and the guide sighed with relief. The *levada* was an awkward spot for an accident that required outside help as no vehicle could reach it.

60

Rhoda, annoyed at her apparent clumsiness and at having become the centre of attention, walked briskly up the steps closely followed by Olga. Fortunately the walk was nearing its end and Rhoda felt sure she could last out the rest without showing the effects of her shaking up. When they reached the road, the taxis were waiting and Olga climbed in with Rhoda. She advised Rhoda to go straight back to the hotel and rest but Rhoda insisted the injury was trivial and stopped with all the other passengers for the usual drink and chat at a bar before going back to their hotels.

'What will you have?' Rhoda's Quinta Magnolia acquaintance was speaking to her.

'A sweet Madeira please Mr . . . I don't know your name.'

'Fred Bradford – call me Fred.'

'Thank you, Fred. I'm Rhoda Brown.'

She sank down with relief on a bench beginning to regret the pride which had made her determined to finish the walk. She had an odd, floating feeling though was not aware of pain.

'Here you are Rhoda.' Fred Bradford deposited her drink and sat down over his beer while Olga hovered anxiously.

'Are you all right, Rhoda?'

'Of course she isn't,' said Fred. 'Nasty shake-up, but she'll be better after a drink.'

Olga gave him a venomous look and ostentatiously walked off to another table. Fred did not seem to notice and after concentrating on his beer, turned to the Dutch lad and started a conversation leaving Rhoda in peace.

She got up rather shakily as the taxi drivers moved firmly to open the doors of their cars as a hint that the excursion was over. Olga got off in the town. Rhoda thought she glimpsed Alec a few yards away. She was glad to see Olga go. She had been very helpful but had she pushed Rhoda on the steps?

Rhoda decided to skip lunch and lie down as soon as she got to her room. She was feeling oddly dizzy and realised she had been silly to have a drink instead of coming straight back. If she was to join Constance and Pixie for tea at Reid's she must have a good rest. Then a shower would revive her. A cut and a bit of bruising was not sufficient excuse for backing out of an engagement or she might have decided to lie down for the rest of the day.

She fell asleep but seemed fully conscious. She was floating in the air looking at the body on the bed. Odd shapes and colours manifested themselves in and out of focus. She tried to wake up to escape the nightmare but when she finally did a couple of hours had passed and she felt far from rested.

She took a shower feeling curiously unco-ordinated all the time. She started to dry herself and wondered why the towel was so wet and saw she had not turned off the water. She did so and took up another towel. What a peculiar colour the ointment was, oozing from under the dressing that Olga had put on the gash in her leg. Everything seemed unnatural. However she felt better for the shower and dressed carefully. When she was ready she found it had taken the best part of an hour and hurried down to meet the others in the lobby. Pixie and Constance were standing near the door.

'How are you? We heard you had an accident on the *levada*.'

Rhoda was always astonished at the speed of gossip. People took such a delight in being associated with even the smallest disaster.

'It was nothing. Just a cut on my leg.'

'We've ordered a taxi to be on the safe side,' said Pixie. 'I expect you have had enough walking for today.'

'That's very thoughtful of you. I am rather tired.'

Rhoda supposed that was what was wrong. She seemed quite dizzy with fatigue. Perhaps she should have had lunch and she certainly should not have had that glass of wine. Tea would be a good thing – they were going to tea, tea at Reid's. She stumbled as she got into the taxi but seeing Pixie and Constance exchanging glances, she pulled herself together.

'It was a splendid walk. I met one of the men I saw at the British Club. His name's Brad Fredford – he's quite a famous naturalist.' Rhoda drivelled on aware that some words were not coming out quite correctly but she must have sounded all right to the others. Anyway the taxi journey was so short that they were concentrating more on having the fare ready than listening to her.

They walked into Reid's, Constance taking the lead as if she were now in her right environment. Rhoda was glad just to follow. She felt as if she were walking a tight rope as she stepped carefully through the chintzy drawing-room, practically hidden behind Pixie's large figure.

The maître d' of teas loomed up and showed them to a table on the crowded terrace. It was a lovely afternoon and a large number of tourists had chosen to commit this particular extravagance as conditions were right. All faces turned towards the newcomers, some with courteous brevity, others openly staring. They loomed up and receded before Rhoda's eyes and she laughed abruptly. They looked so comical with their mouths wide open and their noses swollen with inquisitiveness. Constance looked up sharply.

'What is amusing you?'

Rhoda couldn't remember and re-arranged her features into solemnity. They were now seated and she looked out over the blue sea in which her father had seen a symbol of eternity. Constance's attention was diverted by the arrival of the cake trolley. It whirled in a kaleidoscope of colour but Rhoda managed to indicate a choice without trying to speak. She would be all right after a cup of tea. Constance officiated at the tea tray as if on a stage and handed Rhoda a cup of straw-coloured liquid. Pixie had been looking round at her neighbours and the view and had noticed nothing amiss. Rhoda concentrated on the tea and felt better briefly.

Pixie and Constance were chatting together with the ease of long friendship recalling incidents and people that Rhoda knew nothing of. She tackled her cake. It was no use; the pastry fork was unmanageable. It enlarged and contracted before her eyes, now concealing the whole cake from her, now so tiny that it could not penetrate the icing. 'I'm Alice in Wonderland,' thought Rhoda. Delighted at having solved the problem of her malaise she laughed abruptly again. Pixie and Constance looked at her, startled and disapproving. 'What big eyes you have, grandmother.' Oh no, she wasn't Red Riding Hood; she was Alice. 'I must find the rabbit hole and go back home.'

The last sentence was said aloud and Rhoda scrambled to her feet to set off, dragging the table cloth so that crockery fell to the floor with a crash. Pixie grabbed Rhoda round the shoulders and turned her towards the door leaving Constance to follow amid the gaping crowd.

'She's had an accident – must be delirious,' said Constance loudly with the dominant instinct to keep up appearances. The OC teas loomed up with an expression of disapproval that put Constance's in the shade. As his face expanded and contracted in front of her, Rhoda gave up. It was hilarious. She laughed and laughed.

For once the maître d' of teas quickened his pace. He almost ran, opening doors and guiding his unwanted clients to the front door. Rhoda trod on air enjoying every moment. She had left her body and was watching their antics from above with Olympian delight. Never had a taxi appeared with such celerity at a whistle from the doorman. The maître d' disappeared to return a majestic presence to the terrace while an underling calmly cleared up and relaid the table ignoring the whole incident. The tourists had all brightened up. Instead of the usual hushed tones at Reid's a lively babble had broken out. Some were even addressing strangers at the next table. The trolley was in constant demand and second pots of tea were ordered. No one was going to leave early that day. The maître d' did what he could to retrieve the correct atmosphere. He stood by the trolley with his eyes fixed above the heads of *hoi polloi* and an expression of disdain on his face but little was achieved. For once it looked as if Reid's had been invaded by a coach party and even the prospect of double charges for double helpings could not compensate for the dignified horror of resident guests in the drawing-room.

Meanwhile, in the taxi, Pixie administered a therapeutic slap on the face to stop Rhoda's laughter. It was hardly needed. Rhoda was no longer finding anything funny. Body and mind reunited, she was feeling far from well. Her leg was not painful but everything else about her was. Her head felt like a balloon at full pressure and waves of nausea swept over her. She was barely aware of Pixie getting her room key and pushing her into the lift leaving Constance to ask the receptionist to get a doctor.

'Won't she sleep it off?' he asked, rashly assuming she was drunk. Constance froze him with a glance and he promptly reached for the telephone.

By the time the doctor arrived Pixie had got Rhoda undressed and in bed. She was bathing her face with cold water when Constance knocked on the door. The little Portuguese doctor had been told he would have a drunk patient on his hands but he was not deceived.

'Drugs?' he asked.

'I don't know,' said Pixie. 'I'm sure she isn't that sort of person.'

The doctor grunted. Like the police he did not believe there was a sort of person who never fell from the straight and narrow. He failed to find anything suggesting drug abuse but the symptoms described certainly suggested a trip. Pixie told him what she had heard of the accident on the *levada* walk.

'But she said it was nothing. Just a cut.'

64

The doctor removed the dressing and saw the colour of the ointment.

'Who on earth put this on?' he asked.

Pixie had no further information.

'What is it?'

'Cocaine,' replied the doctor curtly. 'This ointment used to be available but the side effects are so unpredictable that it was withdrawn even from prescription some years ago. Someone must have hung on to old stock.' The doctor asked what tour Rhoda had been on and, as Pixie was able to tell him, he decided to get in touch with the guide before reporting the matter.

'Should I stay with her tonight?' The doctor glanced at the twin beds, Rhoda being one of those who had to pay a massive single room supplement for a great deal of space and furniture she did not need.

'It might be as well, though she will probably sleep through the night now and feel better in the morning.'

'Shouldn't we get a nurse?' asked Constance who did not want her friend associated with Rhoda.

'None available,' said the doctor curtly. 'Not necessary. I'll call again tomorrow. She'll be all the better for a day in bed.' He withdrew hastily, having recognised in Constance the English lady abroad who expected foreigners to carry out her orders. Constance turned angrily to Pixie,

'We should have insisted on professional help. Her travel insurance would surely cover the cost of a nurse.'

'Hush, she might hear,' though as they were standing by the door they were a good distance from Rhoda's bed near the window. 'If it's not necessary, we shouldn't demand it.' Pixie was quite capable of holding her own on matters of principle. 'I'll come along to dinner and then come back here. I expect we shall see someone we know who can keep you company in the evening.'

'You know they'll only want to gossip. It will be all over the hotel that we've been associating with a drug addict.'

'What does that matter as long as it isn't true? Just say that Rhoda was given the wrong drug and is suffering from side effects. You can't stop those who want to make a sensational story of it but something else will happen tomorrow and the scandalmongers will turn in hot pursuit of the newest sensation.'

'If only it hadn't happened at Reid's.' Constance gave away the true foundation of her desire to dissociate herself from Rhoda. 'We shall never be able to go there to tea again.'

'Well, not this holiday,' agreed Pixie regretfully, 'and I had been looking forward to it. It was such a lovely view and the décor reminded me of the old days when we used to go to tea at the Ritz. You go along and change dear. I'll come in half an hour and we can go straight in to dinner. I shan't bother to change as I put on this silk for tea.'

Constance went over to Rhoda.

'She *does* look ill.'

'Yes, well the cocaine must have got into the bloodstream with all the walking she did. It doesn't always pay to have a stiff upper lip even if you don't go to the daft lengths of the Spartans.'

'It's all very strange.' Constance wanted to continue gossiping about the affair with her friend though she intended to keep up appearances before strangers.

'Do go on,' said Pixie with unaccustomed lack of patience. In her way she was as conventional as Constance and had not enjoyed her part in the scene at Reid's. Looking back she could see how ludicrous they must have appeared and she did not appreciate being a target of laughter or scandal any more than Constance.

Constance finally departed leaving Pixie rather ashamed of her irritability. She tidied the room and sat down for a while looking for something to read. She noticed a little brown leather-covered book on the bedside table but, on opening it, saw it was written by hand and therefore private. It was not worth settling down to anything and as soon as the half-hour struck she went down to join Constance for dinner.

It was as they feared. As soon as they reached the bar a couple of complete strangers approached them.

'How is your friend?'

Constance would have frozen them out, but Pixie knew better than to promote uninformed gossip by denying information.

'Much better, thank you,' she said briskly. 'The doctor thinks she will be all right after a day in bed.'

The woman had her mouth open for the next question before Pixie finished speaking but Pixie had not lived all her life in a village for nothing. She had spotted the Grantleys at the other end of the bar and was moving towards them as she concluded the sentence. Short of tripping her up or calling after her the couple

were stymied for the present. The Grantleys were too well man-
nered to ask questions though they had heard the gossip at the
bar. Frank got their drinks and Harriet began a gentle stream of
information about how they had spent their day, leaving it to the
others to begin on their troubles if they wished. Harriet tided them
over until they were all four at their dinner table when even the
most brash were unwilling to approach them, holding their fire till
they withdrew into the lounge for coffee. The curious were frus-
trated as they decided to have coffee at the table and the Grantleys
left the hotel for their apartment immediately after seeing Constance
and Pixie to the lift.

They had told the Grantleys all they knew of Rhoda's catastrophe.
Frank and Harriet had managed to suppress all sign of amusement
at Constance's appalled account of the scene at Reid's though they
shared an appreciative twinkle with Pixie. Constance was a good
raconteur but her bewildered,

'Why did she want to find a rabbit hole?' nearly overcame them.

'Alice in Wonderland?' said Harriet. 'I expect she was brought
up on it. Her education seems to have been a full generation behind
the times.'

Constance stared, unenlightened.

'Drugs can have the effect of strange dreams,' Harriet explained.
'The nightmare quality of some of Alice's experiences would be
suggested by hallucinations.'

'You have experience with drug addicts?' Constance managed to
convey incredulity and disapproval.

'Oh no, but having had children we found it advisable to get to
know enough to recognise symptoms; not in my own children,' she
hastened to add, 'but one needed to separate them from undesirable
friends who got caught up and we heard a good deal about the
effects of misuse. I hadn't realised cocaine was ever used for cuts
but of course it would dull the pain and if the patient remained
still it would not circulate. Rhoda's symptoms were due to her
having been treated in the middle of a walk. Who gave her the
ointment?'

'We don't know. She made light of the accident and we really
did not know what a nasty gash she had until the doctor came. I
thought she must have banged her head and the light headedness
was delirium after concussion.'

'Well I thought she'd been drinking,' said Constance bitterly.

67

'She probably had a drink at the end of the walk.' Frank had been on guided *levada* walks and knew the routine. 'It's usual to have a sociable round at a bar before the party breaks up and that would have added to the trouble.'

Harriet offered to call in at the hotel on the morrow so that Pixie should not feel tied and this offer had been accepted with gratitude. When they got back to their room, Constance commented on the difference between the Grantleys and the other guests.

'The Grantleys know Rhoda personally. The others don't. What they don't know they invent. Remember how it went round the village that the Bell-Wrights were Arab terrorists when they first came all because someone had seen a man with a turban get off the same train when they arrived.'

'Yes, he was going to a UNO meeting and got off at the wrong station. Jones, the taxi, cleared up the rumour eventually.'

'He had to drive the Arab on to Stoneham.'

'I shouldn't be surprised if he started the rumour. Jones has a streak of mischief in his make-up.'

'And the Arab was a Sikh!'

This exchange of recollections brought back the undemanding atmosphere of friendship dating back to schooldays. The friction of present circumstances could not undermine that for long.

'I'll just get my night things together and go along to Rhoda's room.'

'I hope you'll sleep well.'

'Oh, I can sleep anywhere. As long as Rhoda doesn't get delirious again, it will be all right.'

Next morning Rhoda woke early and looked in bewilderment at the occupant of the next bed. She was feeling more or less normal but it took a little time to recall the confusion and distress of the previous day. She felt relieved to think there was no need to cope with anything today. She could stay in her own room and see no one. She turned over and went to sleep again. She woke next time to see Pixie dressed and ready to depart.

'I hope I didn't wake you. It's eight o'clock and Constance and I usually have breakfast about this time. You're looking better. Shall I ring for yours?'

'Yes, please. I feel quite hungry.'

'Well, you've missed a couple of meals so you are ready for something.'

When Rhoda's coffee and rolls appeared, brought by a waiter who showed no consciousness of anything untoward having happened, Constance left saying she would be back in a couple of hours. After breakfast Rhoda had a shower and went back to bed. Her leg was painful but otherwise she felt quite well but tired and decided lying down would be preferable to getting dressed.

Constance and Pixie appeared at ten o'clock and the doctor soon afterwards. Rhoda, who had been scarcely conscious of his previous visit, wanted to know the cause of her illness. The doctor had rung up the guide and been told she was not responsible for the first aid. Now Rhoda was able to tell him about Olga's assistance. The doctor did not need much persuasion that a report to the police was unnecessary. As no one wanted trouble with tourists, he was ready to agree that the incident could be overlooked provided the rest of the ointment was returned to him. Pixie ensured that a correct receipt was exchanged for his fee so that Rhoda could claim from insurance but Rhoda decided in her own mind that it was worth the money to forget the whole thing. She hated filling in forms.

The others left her to rest in peace and the next interruption was a visit from Olga, whose instinct was to exculpate herself by blaming Rhoda for not going straight back to the hotel to rest. Rhoda knew there was some justice in this but was not inclined to let Olga get off blame for administering a banned ointment.

'How did you get hold of it?'

'A friend gave it to me. She had used it herself and found it a good thing. I'd no idea it was banned. In any case, just look at the stuff that's banned, half of it absolutely harmless as long as it's properly used. Our orphanage used to reek of camphorated oil during the winter and now you can't get it because some fatheads drank it instead of rubbing it on their chests.'

Rhoda felt there was some foundation for Olga's argument and certainly the gash on her leg was showing signs of healing already, so she contented herself with telling Olga to let her have the rest of the ointment to return to the doctor. She then invited her to join her for coffee on the balcony.

Olga had either not heard about the extent of the fracas at Reid's or deliberately avoided the subject and as this was what Rhoda wished to do herself they had quite a companionable half-hour. Rhoda took the tray to put it outside the door and when she returned reminded Olga about bringing in the ointment. She noticed Olga had a black look and wondered that she should take offence over what had already been agreed. Still, Olga's moods were unpredictable and she did promise to return later in the day.

'You can leave it at the desk,' suggested Rhoda, thinking Olga might have an engagement with Alec and not want the interruption of a second visit to her.

'I shall put it in your hands.'

Rhoda ignored the snappy tone and said goodbye calmly, thereby irritating Olga the more. However, she was now used to her moods and showed no awareness of a change of atmosphere.

When Olga had left, Rhoda decided to get up and dress. She looked around for a book to take on the balcony and noticed her father's diary was no longer on the bedside table. Pixie must have tidied it away. Several things were out of place but she didn't feel like exerting herself to restore her usual arrangements. She went out on the balcony to enjoy 'a voiceless, dreamless paradise'.

She was awakened by a knock on the door and thought Olga must have come straight back, but this time it was Harriet with a book and a welcome air of normality.

'I see I'm not visiting the sick.'

'No thank you. I'm quite all right now. Would you like to have lunch with me here?'

'I should, very much. Frank is having a business lunch today so I am on my own.'

Her company was very restful. They talked of gardens, of books, of plays, with no personalities to jar and with agreement or disagreement expressed without rancour. It was the most civilised hour that Rhoda had yet spent in Madeira and she felt lucky to have made Harriet's acquaintance. They parted after lunch with mutual goodwill and Rhoda was ready to settle down to the book Harriet had brought her. She spent the afternoon reading *The Age of Innocence*.

Early in the evening Olga called in with the ointment and showed a tendency to linger. She wandered about the room restlessly as if wanting to say something but finally took her departure.

Rhoda decided to have a sandwich in her room in lieu of dinner. When she got into bed she noticed her father's diary was on the bedside table and wondered how she had missed seeing it earlier. It must have fallen behind the table and the maid turning down

70

the bed had put it back. She felt suddenly overcome with fatigue and was glad to have finished the day.

Chapter 9

Pale With Evening

The next day Rhoda was perfectly recovered except for her leg. With the wound unhealed she would not be able to take her swim nor did she feel much inclined to walk. She decided to take her book and lounge by the swimming pool.

She had no sooner settled herself comfortably than the couple who had been balked in their scandal hunt the previous evening came up.

'Are you better?' said the woman. 'We heard you had been poisoned.'

'I am quite well thank you and I have not been poisoned.'

'Oh, is it true you were drugged then?'

'Thank you for your enquiry. I am quite well. Good morning.'

They were quite impervious to a snub. The man took over.

'Is there anything I can bring you? I see there is something the matter with your leg.'

Rhoda got up, put on her bathing robe and walked away.

'Very stand offish, isn't she?' said the woman loudly. 'I suppose she's got a hangover.'

Nearly everyone looked up as Rhoda passed and she was shocked by the avid expressions of curiosity on the faces of people she had seen coming and going in the hotel, apparently ordinary human beings. She got to the lifts and while she was waiting another woman came up to her. This was too much.

'I don't wish to talk . . .' and met the startled glance of Martha Wood, who was standing beside her.

'I'm sorry. I heard you had had an accident and called to . . .'

'Bless you.' Rhoda interrupted her, clutched her arm. 'Do come up to my room. I must talk to someone.'

'But I thought you said you didn't . . .'

'I'll explain when we get to my room.'

When they got there Rhoda rang room service for coffee but after it had arrived her hands shook so much that she couldn't pour it out.'

'Let me do that.' Martha took over efficiently. 'Now tell me what's wrong.'

Rhoda described briefly what had happened the previous day but could not communicate adequately the appalling malice of the encounter at the swimming pool.

'They were complete strangers,' she said more than once.

'The sort that scandal sheets are written for or who ring up people to say their child is dead after a kidnapping. You need not take any notice. The next murder or fire or aeroplane crash and they'll be off in another direction.'

'I don't think I can stand it.'

'Haven't you anyone you can ask to join you here? That type thinks a woman alone is fair game. A companion would help you choke them off.'

Rhoda thought longingly of Matthew Davenport. In Switzerland he had been on the spot and a tower of strength over her accident there. But she would not be able to tell him she thought she had been pushed at the steps. The same type of accident would be too much of a coincidence.

'I know,' said Martha. 'Come with me to Machico. I'm making it my centre for two or three days and there's a marvellous hotel there. If there's a room and the weather holds you can come out with me each day. I *always* work alone so no one can bother you there and when you come back it will all be forgotten.'

'Won't I be in your way?'

'Not a bit. I know from Switzerland that you are capable of amusing yourself. You can read or write letters or whatever while I am sketching. It will give your leg a rest as I shan't be going far or will take a taxi if I do and I'll be glad of your company for meals at the hotel.'

Rhoda needed no further urging. Martha offered to ring up the hotel straightaway so that Rhoda would arrive with her. If any rumours had reached Machico, coming with someone already booked would dissociate her from them.

'Single room,' said Martha triumphantly. 'We'll go tomorrow. Come out to lunch with me now and we'll arrange a group for dinner that will keep the vulgar at bay.'

Rhoda was much cheered and, though they saw a few familiar faces in the restaurant they chose, no one intruded on them. Rhoda enjoyed the meal having been on rather short commons for two days. Martha went back to the hotel with her and they ran into Pixie and Constance. Martha explained why they wanted to make up a party for dinner. Constance had no doubt of her ability to keep the vulgar at bay and said she would ring up the Grantleys. The group would be large enough to repel boarders.

Rhoda did not much want a formal dinner having had a good lunch but she appreciated the efforts made on her behalf and dressed in her best. She looked notably elegant. Even Martha had made an effort and was wearing a shapeless silk instead of a shapeless cotton, clothes for her being intended for warmth and decency. She came up to Rhoda's room to go down in the lift with her ready to put down any approach by strangers. At least they were not bothered by reporters here. The local paper would print nothing reflecting on tourists, hotels, or *levada* walks.

The Grantleys were waiting in the lobby and Frank walked with Rhoda to the bar without reluctance. She was appreciably the most handsome and distinguished-looking lady of her age group. Pixie and Constance were already at the bar and the group had coalesced when Rhoda caught sight of Fred Bradford and his wife. She went over to them and, finding they had intended to dine at this hotel as a change from their usual evening rendezvous with the Wintons, asked them to join her party. Frank Grantley welcomed another man with some relief and, though Mary Bradford's northern accent jarred on Constance, she welcomed Rhoda's initiative as a sign of returning stability. Mary and Pixie obviously hit it off from the beginning and were soon deep in the respective merits of WI and Soroptimists. In the middle of a group of eight, Rhoda was inaccessible to scandalmongers and those who showed signs of trying to join the party lost their nerve before so many cold stares.

A waiter came up to tell them their table was ready and they swept off, en masse, to the dining room. The head waiter, assuming some celebration was in progress, met them gracefully and led them to a beflowered table. The impromptu dinner party proved remarkably successful. It was astonishing what good food, wine and company could do for the morale, thought Rhoda, as she looked round the restaurant. Instead of feeling hunted, she was now a target of envy to others in their usual couples or foursomes, rather bored with themselves and their inevitable companions. She had always noticed in France the difference between the free-flowing conversation of native couples at dinner and the few desultory remarks of English ones. She was delighted to see her party so evidently enjoying themselves, at home in their company and environment.

Fred Bradford had the main attention of the head waiter. Constance was surprised. Frank Grantley was to her the first gentleman of the group, but Fred's outgoing personality would always take the lead wherever he was and Rhoda decided Mary Bradford was the dominant character among the women. Perhaps this was due to the fact that they were themselves on all occasions without the heavy overlay of convention that marked all the others to a greater or lesser degree. They were confident of their own worth and needed no social masks. When it came to the end of the meal Rhoda managed to sign the bill but Fred, with northern generosity, had dealt with the wine waiter and the tips.

Over coffee in the lounge, conversation was general for a time as the party filled a corner to form a coterie cut off from the other guests. Rhoda, who had been the centre of attention, now relaxed with Martha Wood and both listened rather than talking themselves. Pixie was being enlightened on the subject of pigeon-fancying by Mary Bradford. The two men were discussing the future of Madeiran business developments and Constance threw in an occasional remark to all in turn more as a social duty than from any real interest in either topic. Rhoda felt a wave of gratitude to them all. Obviously they were enjoying themselves but they had initially, though comparative strangers, set out to restore her confidence and they had succeeded. The morning's ghastly experience had receded as a nightmare does when one wakes and a feeling of well-being swept over her as she looked at her companions.

When the party broke up, promises of information to be exchanged, books to be lent, expeditions to be shared, showed a degree of bonhomie among all. They would be around still when

75

Martha and Rhoda returned from Machico and it was agreed that the same party should dine together again.

It was only ten o'clock when Rhoda got back to her room. She felt so revived that she decided to ring up Matthew Davenport, her friend made on the Swiss holiday. She would tell him something of what had happened and hoped that, combined with her enthusiasm for Madeira, he might be tempted to come out for a few days.

She got through with what always seemed to her extraordinary ease and clarity. After exchanging greetings Davenport asked what was wrong.

'How could you tell something was wrong?'

'I'd have had a letter not a phone call if everything was going smoothly.'

'The trouble is something similar to what happened in Switzerland. I have had an accident – no nothing serious – but with unpleasant consequences and I can't be sure it was entirely an accident.'

'And you'd like me to come and find out?'

Rhoda appreciated the quick response to her implicit appeal and agreed his presence would be a comfort.

'Can you really drop everything?'

'I'm retired – nothing I do is essential – if it ever was,' replied Davenport cheerfully. 'I'll see you if I can get a flight and ring you tomorrow evening.'

Rhoda recalled she would be in Machico and gave him the phone number of the hotel and recounted the coincidence of meeting Martha Wood in the British Cemetery.

'The flower lady?'

'Yes, it was she who suggested I should join her in Machico for a few days to get away from the gossip in the hotel.'

'You'll be all right then, I remember her as a "no nonsense and get on with the job" person. Good – I'll be in touch. Take care, whatever that absurd idiom is intended to convey.'

Rhoda put the phone down and laughed. The conversation had succeeded in reducing the events of the last two days to their rightful proportions. She went to bed and slept soundly. She had notified the hotel and her courier that she would be away for a few days but wanted to retain her room and leave most of her luggage so that she could return when she wished.

Next morning she had only to pack. Martha Wood picked her up in a taxi and Rhoda sat back with a sigh of relief to enjoy the winding route with its verges of flowers and shrubs. Martha told her she intended to book in and set off immediately to a site already fixed on for her first day's work in the neighbourhood. Rhoda said she would settle in at the hotel at leisure and was not averse to temporary solitude. On their arrival they went their separate ways. Rhoda unpacked and settled down to look at the view from her window – similar to but less extensive than that in Funchal.

Chapter 10

Voice of Broken Seas

The relief of escaping from Funchal was inexpressible. Matthew Davenport would phone that evening and meanwhile the retirement into comparative rural peace among people who had come primarily to enjoy it was restorative. She went down to lunch in an almost empty dining-room. Of the tables occupied, several were assigned to elderly single ladies. Rhoda guessed them to be retired teachers exorcising a lifetime of dinner duties. They spent a couple of hours over lunch enjoying to the full the four separate courses and the full attention of two or three waiters. They spoke little. Silence at a meal after their experiences was a pleasure; to be responsible for no one but themselves, ecstasy. No one could enjoy the negative freedom from responsibility for others with the positive delight of ex-school teachers. Herself having been educated by a governess, Rhoda had read Vera Britain and others of the post First World War generation whose talents had been crushed by the sheer physical weariness of working in potty little private boarding schools. Only then could they gain the experience without which they could not get a job in a school with reasonable educational standards.

Rhoda's thoughts had wandered thus far when she realised the presence of another phenomenon. She and other single women were sitting alone at tables overlooking the bay. This must be the only hotel in the world that accorded such privileges to the single and elderly though Rhoda herself was a good decade short of the latter. She wondered what combination of circumstances had led to this unique feature among hotels. Perhaps Portugal retained the family values, lost elsewhere in affluent Europe, which had an integral place in society for every age group. Yet there had been an old woman in black outside the hotel with hand held out and a beggar's whine. Still that was better than groups of youths loafing about, their future void, matching their empty pasts.

With a feeling of well-being which she had missed since the *levada* incident, Rhoda returned to her room. She stretched out on her bed, adjusted the pillows and settled down to an old Margery Allingham. Here there would be a narrative without boring interpolations of sex and violence to break the sequence and recall the disagreeable realities one came on holiday to forget. So reading she drifted into a comfortable doze, waking conveniently at a time appropriate for tea.

As soon as she entered the lounge she was incorporated in a cosy group ready to accept a new guest as an enlivening incident.

> Arriving we began a busy chat
> On politics and weather, this and that.

The men were ready to discuss with a newcomer what they had read in a day-old newspaper. The women were eager to instruct on the services of the hotel and the discovery of unexpected bargains in the shops. It was restful even to return to a generation that provided different roles for men and women. Rhoda had long deplored the use feminists made of new-found liberation to go on doing the daft things that men had wasted time and resources on for centuries. No one learns from the experience of others. Sipping straw-coloured tea and eating exceptionally good toast, Rhoda listened with pleasure to conversation devoid of sensation as it flowed on without any effort on her part except the occasional murmur of agreement.

After tea she strolled through the village and, recalling the holiday obligation of sending post cards, she bought a few. Writing these would occupy her till dinnertime by which time Martha would have returned and a mildly sociable evening would provide an agreeable conclusion to a restful day.

In Machico, she discovered, instead of human Artful Dodgers, there were canine ones. Undeterred by her insulting 'Scat!' one attached itself to her, either behind or in front, but she did not succeed in jettisoning it till, getting to the hotel, it curled up on her doorstep to await its next victim. Was it trained to annoy or did it hope to find an owner? Presumably there were holidaymakers here as in England cruel enough to encourage its advances and then abandon it without thought when they returned home.

Seated in the hotel lounge with a view of the bay to provide inspiration, Rhoda wrote with enthusiasm about everything in Madeira except her personal experiences. A few minutes only were needed to get ready for dinner as Martha never bothered with dress and Rhoda did not want to provide a contrast. They met at the bar and had a quick drink as Martha was more than ready for dinner, having had nothing but a sandwich through the day. It had been a profitable day's work and she reckoned one more would provide all she needed for this region so Rhoda decided to accompany her on the morrow. Martha was ready for an early night so both went to their rooms after coffee, Martha to sleep the sleep of the just and Rhoda to await Matthew Davenport's phone call.

It came through quite early.

'All Sir Garnet,' he said immediately. 'I've got a flight for the day after tomorrow.'

'That's perfect. Martha thinks she will finish here tomorrow and she doesn't want to linger at a place when she'd finished work there so she will be able to go on the north of the island without thinking she has deserted me.'

'Good, then I'll come to Machico from the airport and we can go to Funchal together after a day or two there. You sound quite different today.'

'Yes, this is a very restful spot and the hotel is largely occupied by senior citizens just now – an agreeable crowd, friendly and undemanding.'

'Well, I should be with you by teatime on Wednesday. The flight is due in the early afternoon and I'll take a taxi. It's no distance from Machico.'

'No, I shall see your plane flying in from my room.'

Goodbyes said, Rhoda rang off with a feeling of satisfaction. If Matthew couldn't solve her problems, at least she could talk about them to him with perfect freedom of understanding and sympathy.

Next day she had to be ready for an early start for Martha had ordered a taxi to take them to a *levada* along which she expected to find the specimens she needed. They took lunch with them for this was not one of the *levadas* where set tourists' walks took place and bars were conveniently placed for refreshment after a couple of hours' walking. Much as she disliked picnics, Rhoda expected to enjoy a day off the beaten track. The walking was much harder than on the guided walks. Paths were rougher and women carrying loads had to be waited for and there were the long intervals when Martha got down to her sketching. Rhoda enjoyed it all, the old men courteously doffing their woollen caps and responding to 'Bon Dia', children grinning amiably, the sight of the intensively cultivated little terraces. It took Rhoda back to walks on the estate in her childhood when she knew everyone and everyone knew her and the courtesies of life were still observed.

The day passed quickly and Martha found at the end that she had achieved what she came for. Aware that Rhoda no longer needed her support she arranged to leave after an early breakfast. They made their farewells after dinner, Rhoda with gratitude and Martha with some relief that it had all worked out so easily and she could proceed to her next site free of any responsibility.

Rhoda was rather pleased to have a morning to herself. She went down to breakfast to find the dining-room empty except for some small groups of Germans and Scandinavians evidently preparing for a strenuous *levada* walk. Here, though alone, she could have a table by the window and look out over the bay, the rising sun producing a pleasant abstract of rose and gold on the horizon. A waiter appeared immediately. The natural warmth of the Portuguese, noticeable even in sophisticated Funchal, was even more evident here and when he enquired 'How did you sleep?' Rhoda had difficulty in restraining herself from describing her restful night. Recalling herself in time to remember that only one's mother is interested in how one has slept (and Rhoda's mother had deputed that duty with practically all other maternal cares to a nannie), Rhoda uttered a noncommital 'Very well, thank you' and proceeded to enjoy coffee and rolls as well as the view. Her cure was complete. She felt assured that dizziness would not return and full enjoyment of the holiday would.

With the inevitable canine attendant, she wandered round the village and viewed the harbour where Zarco made his first landing. How fortunate that it was the Portuguese who had 'discovered' Madeira. They could bring a leisured good humour to match the mild climate. A light lunch and Rhoda had nothing to do but wait for the arrival of the afternoon plane.

Her current book had not the grip of *Staying On* but it filled the time till she changed into the latest triumph of her home boutique at Stoneborough. She had retained her figure and the dark brown of her hair and could look distinguished in a plain linen dress remarkably well cut and finished for contemporary fashion, meriting the sort of price which TV fashion programmes claimed without such qualities. She did not see the taxi arrive but in any case had the tact to remain in her room until Davenport rang through to announce his arrival, having had time to recover from the fatigue of crowded aeroplane travel.

They shook hands at the reception desk, neither of them having any use for the irrelevant intimacies that compel prizewinners to accept embraces from repellent celebrities. They went out on to the terrace overlooking the swimming pool, deserted at that time as the sun had disappeared behind the hill overshadowing the hotel. They ordered tea and toast, which, crisp and buttery, was to Rhoda one of the triumphs of their cuisine, having little taste for elaborate sauces obscuring good food.

The first cups of tea poured, Davenport remarked, 'You don't look any the worse for your injury.'

'No, the cut on my leg has almost healed.' She indicated the scar with the surrounding bruise, now more yellow than blue. 'I'm sorry I panicked and virtually blackmailed you into making this trip but the whole thing was a nightmare.'

'Oh, I'm glad to see the island again and I've reached the age when it's no hardship to escape a few days of the English winter.'

Rhoda looked at him gratefully. This was friendship, a relationship between man and woman which the modern novelist seemed never to have observed let alone experienced.

'Well?'

'It's difficult to distinguish between fact and the effects of the drug. The doctor said that the ointment Olga Bayne put on the cut was cocaine-based and was bound to enter the bloodstream and cause hallucinations. But why should anyone do that to me?'

Davenport looked mildly amused. Rhoda's unconscious air of distinction and self-sufficiency could easily inspire an act of spite from someone resentful of such qualities and since the break-up of the approximately egalitarian society established after the Second

World War, such resentment was in the air. Money could be acquired like waste paper but the arrived air of a place in society was not so attainable even by those who could afford the services of the new generation of butlers. Rhoda looked enquiringly but Matthew merely said,

'You've had time to think it over now. Tell me all about it from the beginning. Remember I don't know the dramatis personae as I did in Switzerland.'

'It happened on one of the regular *levada* walks. You know how you get the occasional bit that needs care – where a channel crosses a path and the rock steps are slippery. Well, I was stepping with great care when I felt a slight push. I slipped and fell. After my experience in Switzerland I couldn't speak of the push to anyone but you. I am still almost certain of it. The only person near enough to have done it was Olga Bayne but though she has a decided chip on the shoulder we had become quite friendly. I invited her to tea after we'd shared a toboggan on an earlier excursion. She told me she had been brought up in an orphanage but she was obviously quite well educated there as she was able to take a job in computers. I rather liked her as her sense of humour seemed to get the better of self-pity. Others came up but Olga had got a first aid case out and I was too shaken to cope for myself. She put this yellow ointment on and stuck a large band aid over it before anyone else had time to comment. We weren't far from the end of the walk and I was able to cover the distance without too much discomfort. Back at the hotel I felt a bit odd but I had promised to go to tea at Reid's with two acquaintances. They are friends who come from the same village and had been to school together. One has an improbable name – Pixie Putley – a jolly extrovert. Her friend, Mrs Constance de Lisle, is a snob of the old school but has her good qualities when you get to know her.'

'As I no doubt shall.'

'Yes, you must meet them. They really stood by me after the catastrophe. They had arranged to take a taxi when they heard I had a fall (really a hotel is as bad as a village for gossip) so I had no good reason to withdraw from the engagement. Anyway after a rest I got up and joined them in the taxi feeling very peculiar but unable to believe it as I could scarcely feel my leg and am not given to fainting or dizzy turns. When we got out of the taxi I felt I should go straight back to the hotel but something seemed to take over my will. Constance de Lisle's disapproving air was natural but I thought Pixie was looking at me oddly. The stately waiter officiating for 'Tea at Reid's' approached and, with Constance in the lead, there was no difficulty about getting a good table on the terrace. I sat down to look over the scene my father had surveyed long before my birth but everything was distorted. Crockery rose and fell, faces loomed up and receded, colours and shapes whirled round me. I heard someone laughing idiotically and knew I was making a scene but it just seemed very funny. The maître d'hotel of teas was bearing down on our table but before he could reach it Pixie has seized me and was hoisting me towards the exit. Constance, endeavouring to look totally detached, diverted the waiter's attention with an excessive tip. Pixie got me into a taxi, the driver evidently enjoying the variety from the usual style of lady leaving Reid's. He rolled his eyes understandingly as Pixie urged him to hurry, 'So drunk, so happy', he seemed to think it a pity to consign me to my room as was Pixie's obvious intention. Constance joined us, wearing now with good reason her normal expression accentuated by the fact she had a fellow-countrywomen, not a foreigner, under her nose. Pixie with more perception was worried. She knew I couldn't be drunk and could recognise drug symptoms from the social work she does even if not professionally trained and she saw me as an unlikely addict. So she got me to my room and rang the desk for a doctor.

'A small, dark-eyed Portuguese who spoke excellent English arrived but though I was aware of his presence I could not communicate. The rest of the interview I got from Pixie later as by then I was really over the top, apparently to the extent of physical hostility towards the doctor. However, when he examined the cut on my leg and saw the ointment he was enlightened. To all intents and purposes I had had a shot of cocaine. He wanted to know who had provided the ointment but Pixie did not know as she had not been on the *levada* walk. He told her the effects would wear off in about twenty-four hours and departed to get in touch with the guide.'

'I suppose the question now is, was the ointment administered in good faith or for some sinister purpose? Who was the good Samaritan?'

'Olga Bayne.'

'Could she have intended it as a practical joke?'

'I wouldn't have thought so. I thought she was pleased to know someone of a higher social class than hers. She's the sort of person Constance de Lisle would not acknowledge with a "Good morning" in the dining room. Not that she's staying at our hotel. She's staying at a hotel in the town. A young man joined her a day or two after we met.'

'Could he be a malign influence? Put her up to it out of sheer devilment?'

'I've seen him only once and that briefly. He looked quite amiable but perhaps weak and shiftless.'

'What is his name?'

'She didn't introduce me to him. She called him Alec which I suppose was all she would have said if she *had* introduced me. The anonymity of forenames seems to be here to stay.'

'Can they be up to something shady together and want to discredit you beforehand as a witness? Have you seen anything suspicious since you've been here?'

'Good heavens, no. They call this place paradise and the activities are as moderate as the climate. The only sign of evil I've seen was the repellent curiosity of some of the hotel guests which led to my escaping here for a day or two and even that was counterbalanced by the kindness and support I got from some of the others whom I've met only since my arrival here. Martha Wood is the only one I knew before.'

'So if it weren't for the fact you thought Miss Bayne pushed you, you might accept the whole affair as fortuitous?'

'I suppose so. Of course in Switzerland I was on the look out for suspicious circumstances . . .' Rhoda stopped suddenly.

'You've thought of something?'

'Yes, but it happened at Faro and can't have anything to do with Olga. We weren't able to land at Madeira and spent a night at Faro. There were two people sitting by me on the plane, very smart, very dull. Our coach departure was delayed a little and I took a stroll in the harbour. I saw these two walking round the harbour in opposite directions and as they passed each other they exchanged briefcases. They did not stop to speak and it struck me as odd but since meeting Mark Pemberley and hearing about the extraordinary experiences of customs officers I'm apt to let my imagination run away with me.'

'Drug smugglers?' Davenport sounded quite serious. 'It's certainly strange. Have you seen anything of them here?'

'I thought I saw the man in the Blandy gardens but I'm not sure I would recognise either of them in different clothes. Their dress was the only distinctive thing about them and I never heard them speak.'

'You've had no connection with them except for sitting by them on the plane?'

'None.'

'Then I don't think that is a significant lead, unless they realised you had noticed the exchange and wanted to discredit a potential witness in advance. It might be worth our while to look out for any indication of a connection between one of them and Olga Bayne so, if you do see either of them again, point them out to me.'

'I wonder if Olga's young man might be the connection. When I was talking to her she quite lit up over the thought of taking a degree and turned dour again. She was dismissed from her post for using the company computer for private purposes. If Alec was associated with her over that, he might have got her involved in some criminal activity which would prevent her from making a fresh start. She obviously has ability but he has never had a steady job, if a steady job is a possibility nowadays.'

'Well, it looks as if we shall have to wait to get back to Funchal to begin looking into things seriously. How long had you planned to stay here?'

'I had no plans when I came other than to get away from intrusive gossips and as soon as I got here they receded into their rightful insignificance. I could go back any time though now I'm here I like the atmosphere so much that I'd like to stay a little longer.'

'Then I'll stay over tomorrow and have a local *levada* walk. I suppose you had better not attempt it with your bad leg?'

Rhoda laughed. The phrase had reduced her to the company of the old women of the village of her childhood.

'The "bad leg" was an almost inevitable topic of conversation when one visited in the village in the old days. I hadn't realised how depreciating it must feel to have always an ailment rather than your personality to the fore.'

'I don't think you need worry in your case. I must have been influenced by the frequency with which I heard the phrase as a small child too. I lived in a village before I went to prep school.'

'I won't attempt a *levada* walk here. The one I saw with Martha was rougher than the guided walks I've done, though I saw very little of it and spent most of the day resting as we didn't have to go far from the taxi for the specimens Martha wanted. I shall be glad when I can get some real exercise. My leg is healing with extraordinary rapidity but it would still be antisocial to use the swimming pool.'

'Let's hope a restful day or two will enable you to get back to holiday activity in Funchal.'

Rhoda had already decided that rest was what she was going to take in Machico so was able to agree with the old-world feminine tact of appearing to accept advice from a man on matters which she had already resolved on herself.

Next morning Rhoda came down a little later than usual in order to breakfast by herself. Davenport had planned the evening before to accompany a group of Scandinavian walkers who were making an early start and she did not want to intrude on a group of hardy activists but would hardly have been able to avoid them if Matthew was one of their number. With relief she found she had landed comfortably between the hearty energetic and the somnolent late risers. A window table was therefore free again and the usual warm enquiry whether she had slept well provided a companionable parenthesis in her solitude without demanding a personal response. The wide bay provided a beautiful background against which the nearer view both human and natural supplied varied vignettes. There were no birds but a solitary leaf floating hither and thither in the wind currents filled the gap. Of blossom there was never a shortage on the island.

On the road below a woman laden with a heavy shopping bag was patiently conducting the first steps of a tiny toddler who stumbled and was immediately received into her mother's arms regardless of the weight of the shopping. Rhoda recalled an unpleasant incident she had once witnessed in England. A child had stopped to gaze entranced into the window of a toy shop. His smartly dressed mother turned to drag him away saying sharply, 'Adrian, haven't you a mind above toys?' He couldn't have been more than three, poor child. What life was there in store for him? This Portuguese child had better prospects though the family income would not be a tenth of the English mother's.

The dining-room was filling up and Rhoda left her table for the

87

benefit of some late riser. A gentle stroll through the village came first on her programme for a restful day. Really to appreciate a rest one must be able to watch other people working. As she walked under the trees she watched the street cleaners. Five women clad in neat beige uniforms leaned on their besoms, chatting, while two others put leaves in a wheelybin. A few yards off another (the forewoman?) screamed volubly but, without Portuguese, Rhoda could not tell whether she was 'tearing off a strip' or dominating the conversation. Anyway the loiterers listened unmoved and returned to their chat so presumably the job was proceeding amicably and at a genuinely human pace.

Significant though, thought Rhoda, that the women have the dull, routine street-cleaning jobs where the men have the varied creative gardening.

She moved on to the sea front and watched the waves wash over the black rocks. The peace was broken by the barking of dogs, 'those lewd, loud-mouthed foes to quiet' as Osbert Sitwell described them. They were certainly one of the very few obtrusively objectionable features of the island. Rhoda withdrew to the swimming pool and found a chair with no immediate neighbour and with the aid of a book passed the time till lunch effortlessly.

There were never many people at lunch so that Rhoda could enjoy her observation platform at the window with a variety of human interest rather different from that at breakfast time. She watched the high-school teenagers assembled at a bench on the front, the girls absorbed in the boys and the boys absorbed in motor bikes. One boy passed on his machine at snail's pace in order to secure his full meed of admiration. A girl flagged him down on the pretext of getting a light for her cigarette – a sad declension from the old days of a dropped handkerchief. And with all the lovely embroidered handkerchiefs on the island it was a pity there was no revival of the ancient method of securing an introduction without the risk of lung cancer or pollution from exhausts. It would provide a pretty scenario to match these vivid dark-eyed girls and boys, not unattractive even in their teens. The boy roared off leaving the girl puffing ineffectually but regarded with envious eyes by her less bold contemporaries.

Though far from tropical, Madeira encouraged the siesta habit and Rhoda soon fell asleep over a Gothic paperback on returning to her room. When she came down to tea she found Davenport already in the lounge sitting with an elderly couple with whom he seemed already on amicable terms. He and the elderly gentleman rose as Rhoda approached and Davenport introduced her to Mr and Mrs Heathcote. The introduction was formal but Matthew immediately went on to say,

'We have adopted the useful holiday anonymity and are using Christian names Rhoda. Agnes and Douglas.' Everyone smiled and conversation flowed freely. Both Heathcotes possessed a sharp wit often exercised on one another but as they were obviously a devoted couple, this practice was not embarrassing to their companions. They were both handsome too which made them pleasant to look at – tall, white-haired, blue eyed – looking rather alike as couples of long standing often do. Their faces were expressive, the lines of personality distinguishing them from the anonymity of old age into which elderly travellers often fall with similarity of clothes, hair styles and topics of conversation. The superficiality of holiday acquaintanceship made people easy to approach but equally easily forgettable. The Heathcotes were different. They had not been chatting five minutes before Rhoda realised she would forget neither of them even if she never saw them again. In fact she found herself hoping that they would find a friend in common with her or Matthew to ensure that they did not lose sight of one another.

No time was spent on weather, shops or news. A book which Douglas had been reading provided interest for all. It had been shortlisted in a literary prize contest and had not won. Douglas was of the opinion that it should have done.

'The winner was one of these episodic, eight-hundred-page ramblings, rightly described as sexy by one of the judges, though what relevance that has with literary criticism I don't know. I read it in paperback and between the difficulty of identifying the characters, most of whom had unpronounceable ethnic names, and the disintegration of the binding which resulted in my reading a number of pages out of order without noticing anything wrong, I failed to finish it.' Agnes had summed up the identifying features of much contemporary writing and printing.

'Bad binding is no more relevant to literary criticism than "sexy",' Douglas pointed out.

'Indeed it is. Where there is no coherence in a book, even its material aspect disintegrates. You can't separate body and spirit. The crazy fashion for novelty means that everything is ephemeral.

Nobody looks beyond today. Take cars. Every family wants two cars in both of which separate individuals sit in traffic jams. Then money. It is so plentiful that inflation increases so that homes no longer exist. Young couples both work to pay a mortgage so large they can't afford children and are seldom in the house to which their lives are being sacrificed.'

Agnes suddenly grinned and Rhoda could see her as the girl Douglas had met half a century before.

'You can see literary criticism is not my strong point. I'm interested in living.'

'You should be an essayist,' said Douglas. 'The essay is due for a revival. It's been lost since the Second World War. I suppose no one dare philosophise on truth now. We should lose all our governments. But you could write them on ephemera.'

'On Civilisation,' suggested Davenport.

'On the Arts,' said Rhoda.

'On Speculation,' from Douglas.

'On Fossil Fuels, on Law and Order. An essay on essay titles would be in keeping with today's episodic approach to everything. No one has the patience to work out anything constructive so bits of patchwork are applied to everything till no foundation is left to work on.' Agnes was getting too serious for tea-table talk and she grinned again and said,

'This isn't the place to talk like this. Madeira has some foundation fabric still left.'

'Yes.' Rhoda had felt this in many ways on the island. 'But it's the old fabric based on the church. What will happen when the European patch covers it?'

'Plenty of awful examples for them to avoid,' Davenport's contribution produced silence as each thought of the particular awful example met on travels.

Another couple came up.

'May we join you?' as they sat down and ordered tea.

It was a tribute to the atmosphere of the hotel that no one had thought this was out of order even though none of them had met the newcomers before. It was more like a club than a hotel.

Marcia and Rupert Wallace were among those for whom book and magazine were synonymous. The publications that entered their house were passed on as soon as glanced through to the hairdresser or dentist for their waiting rooms. They would never have to face the problems of what to do with the furniture when bookcases covered the walls of every room. The Heathcotes, however, were in no way disconcerted by the complete re-orientation of the conversation. They were interested in people and the detachment of hotel holidays enabled them to meet a wide variety without the problem of ever having to meet them again unless they really wanted to.

The Wallaces proved to be food fanatics. Rhoda preferred these to wine connoisseurs whom she found affected both in taste and, what was worse, in language. After all food was a necessity of life and it was a good thing that some people were unashamed of their pursuit of it. Since Madeira supplied a variety of restaurants the Heathcotes were soon into as lively a conversation as they had been with Rhoda and Davenport. Rhoda was glad when an interval came and she and Matthew could politely break away to have a stroll before dinner.

When they reached a seat overlooking the sea heaving over the black rocks they sat down to talk in comfort. Rhoda disliked trying to talk as one wandered in occupied places, words carried away by the noise of traffic or interrupted by manoeuvring round passers by. They had become accustomed to walking silently.

'Did you enjoy your walk this morning?'

'It was a bit strenuous for me but there's always satisfaction in being able to keep up with the youngsters. And Scandinavians generally speak such good English that one can enjoy the company without the strain of thinking in a foreign language. We were late back as we spent a long time in the bar we stopped at on the way home.'

'I like that custom. It's nice to have plenty of people to talk to without being involved with them.'

Matthew smiled. He was by now well aware of Rhoda's detached attitude to society. He put it down to her having been born an only child to rather elderly parents. She had a unique place in the world from the beginning and felt no desire or obligation to share it. She was an ideal companion for Davenport whose brief marriage in youth, sadly cut short by his wife's death in a car accident, had left him to a single life to which, as an Oxford don, there was every opportunity to adapt himself.

'I shall go to Funchal tomorrow. I booked in at Reid's for that date and though I'd like to stay on here I think I'll keep to the booking. If I meet any of your acquaintances, it might be helpful to see them on my own. I'll drop in at your hotel for a drink before dinner and if I can pick up Miss Putley and Mrs de Lisle I can cross them off the list of suspects.'

Rhoda laughed. 'They are the last people I'd put on it but you might enjoy meeting them. They are decided characters if not as interesting as the Heathcotes.'

'Yes, I'd like to meet the Heathcotes again. I'll see if they intend to go to Funchal in the next few days and we'll arrange to meet them. You'll be coming the day after tomorrow?'

'I shall. Two flights have left for Gatwick while I've been here so I hope the worst of the intruders at my hotel will have gone and I shall be left in peace.'

'Don't worry, something new will have arisen to attract their attention. That type hasn't more than a twenty-four hour attention span even for scandal.'

'True, but I hadn't met it before and I hope I never shall again.'

The Heathcotes were dining at the hotel and Davenport and Rhoda joined them. The Wallaces were trying out a new restaurant so the others were able to discuss the book that had not won the literary prize and the author would have been cheered had he been able to hear their discussion and verdict. The conversation wandered from books to theatre and a measure of agreement in principle, with differences of opinion in detail, ensured a congenial colloquy for their last dinner together in Machico.

Chapter 11

They Who Believed in Friends

Rhoda sacrificed the bliss of solitude to have breakfast with Davenport before he left for Funchal. Perhaps it was no kindness to him accustomed to the unsociable taciturnity of high-table breakfast in an Oxford college but she was rather dismayed to find she still needed the assurance of the presence of a true friend. It was an unnatural coincidence to have another accident on holiday in which she was doubtful whether there had been an assailant. A wall in the citadel of her self-sufficiency had been breached and Matthew's welcoming smile as she joined him was a brick in its restoration.

'I'll anticipate the waiter and ask if you slept well?' he said.

'Don't they do it well? When they ask if you've enjoyed your coffee they sound as if they mean it and would be disappointed if you said no. I have never been in any other hotel where the insincere courtesies of waiters sounded so genuine.'

'Perhaps they are. They seem happy in their work here.'

'Yes. One of the waiters burst into song the other day. Was it an expression of spontaneous joy or was he practising for his night job? I gather a lot of hotel staff double as entertainers on their nights off.'

'Don't be cynical. They may be able to combine pleasure and work in a way most other Europeans have lost, except perhaps the French, who have clung to their two-hour lunch break with persevering civilisation.'

'Unlike the English "weekend" which had become an objective in itself towards which you scramble through the working week.'

The waiter arrived with more coffee and a beaming smile.

'The coffee is good?'

'Splendid.' Rhoda found herself using superlatives in response to all this good will though she normally deplored the advertising industry's misuse of language which first depreciates language and then diminishes the values it expresses. She thought of the use of 'conventional' for non-nuclear weapons. Her father had been horrified by the damage human beings inflicted on one another at Chitral. She was thankful he had died before the Second World War. How could he have lived in an age when the weapons of mass destruction had become a convention, unquestioned and accepted because they were not nuclear and because those who authorised their use might escape undamaged themselves.

They had drunk the last cup of coffee in silence.

'A penny . . .?'

'No, Matthew. I refuse to pursue the horrors of civilisation at breakfast. When is your taxi ordered for?'

'Not till the middle of the morning. We've time for a stroll in the village. I expect you will be up to a *levada* walk by the time you get back to Funchal. I'll arrange one instead of going on a guided one and then you can give it up if you find it too much.'

'I'll be quite ready for walks but the cut, though healing well, is still too conspicuous on my leg for swimming. It will need two or three more days for that.'

They wandered through the village and on to the front with the inevitable canine attendant and the resulting bursts of barking when they passed a house.

'I've been thinking, Rhoda. You told me your father kept a diary in Madeira. If it is not too personal would you let me read it?'

'Of course. But it was written so long ago that it can have no relevance to anything happening now though it is interesting that we can still enjoy some of the activities that he did. His India has disappeared. Did I ever tell you that it was reading Paul Scott's *Staying On* that made me decide on coming to Madeira? There was always an association of surviving an era in connection with my father. He was not a twentieth-century man though most of his life was lived in it. Perhaps survival is not the right word for he was not altogether a nineteenth-century man either. Perhaps the element of the nineteenth century in which he lived was that which led to Tennyson's use of the Arthurian legends – a beautiful, sad, phantom

94

world, whose unreality could not accept death. My governess read a lot of Tennyson with me and, while I enjoyed the perfection of words, I was jarred by the remoteness from real life. When I came to read Mallory I realised why. There is a total absence of humour. The only approach to humour I remember was a pun. Coming across a tough opponent at the feast following a joust, Sir Lancelot said, "I hope I shall never meet you again except at a dish of meat." Then he laughed so much at his own joke that he fell off the bench. Poor Guinevere!'

'Yes the medieval period was tough on women in royal circles. A middle-class woman who inherited her husband's business was in the best position to enjoy that era.'

Davenport's taxi was soon due and they returned to the hotel. Rhoda went to her room to get the diary and, giving it to him, said,

'I'm afraid you won't find it as interesting as his letters.'

'Possibly not but I appreciate you lending it to me and I'll return it tomorrow.'

Davenport was more interested in the influence the long dead father had over Rhoda than in the contents of the diary but, as it happened, it gave him the first lead to understanding the odd attack on Rhoda. Meanwhile he pocketed it and said goodbye.

Rhoda turned back into the hotel with a sense of loss. She had many friends and acquaintances but none so companionable as he. Perhaps it was because he was the only one who could meet her on even terms in the world of books. She had never made an allusion which he was not able to pick up. It was the first time that Rhoda had found a kindred spirit in the book world and coming late in life she valued it greatly. Had she gone to university such friends would have belonged to her youth but her sociable mother had never bothered with books beyond making sure she heard of any that were currently making a mark. She had subscribed to Mudie's to its end and then to Boots till the library ended and then had ceased to read, getting the necessary information to be up with fashion from TV or the men who flocked round her all her life. It had puzzled Rhoda that her father had married a society woman but she had decided by observation that the attraction of opposites was the basis of many marriages.

She met the Wallaces on their way out to a taxi which was to carry them to yet another restaurant for lunch and seeing her alone asked her if she would like to join them. Rhoda accepted the invitation thinking a gourmet lunch would pass the time since she would be unable to swim. The Wallaces were pleasant people without having the tiresome marital habit of so many couples of correcting detail in the partner's narrative to the extent that it ruined conversation.

The taxi carried them a good distance north and, as this was new territory to Rhoda, she enjoyed the drive. The meal was excellent and returning appropriately at four o'clock they had tea together with the Heathcotes. They exchanged news of their day and invited Rhoda to have dinner with them but one large meal was enough and Rhoda declined as she would be packing for her return to Funchal the next day.

'I expect we shall see you there soon,' said Agnes. 'We arranged with Matthew Davenport to have tea at Reid's one day and assumed you would come too.'

'That will be delightful.'

Rhoda's response was an automatic courtesy. She was by no means sure that she ever wanted to enter Reid's again. The memory of the horrible hallucinations she had suffered and the even more horrible memory of having made a scene in public were sufficient to deprive the prospect of another tea at Reid's of any attraction. It might be a good thing on the principle of getting back on the horse you have fallen from but she could not look forward to it with any pleasure. However, she was well aware that while one is the centre of one's own world one is peripheral to others. If not forgotten her unfortunate experience would no longer be of interest, having been fully talked out by now and losing its attraction in her absence. There is all the difference in gossip from being able to begin,

'Do you see that woman over there? Well . . .' and 'There was a woman staying here who . . .'

The illusion that long stories about people not known even by name or sight can hold interest was not one to which gossips are subject. They are quick to spot the glazed eye and wandering attention of their vis-à-vis. Hence the passion to be able to say they have spoken to the victim, for that is the only word for the subject of gossip. What is known will be exaggerated and what is not known will be invented. The whole is never known to the victim except by the effects. Rhoda was fortunate in never having needed a job to live by so her character could be clouded without economic disaster. And for friends, the acid test was their reception of gossip.

Anyone who believed or spread it could be dropped by Rhoda without diminishing the quality of her life. In the world of work this is impossible.

Counting her blessings, Rhoda went to spend a quiet evening in her room.

Meanwhile Davenport had arrived at Reid's and was enjoying the old-fashioned décor combined with modern comfort. He was old enough to feel the effects of his long walk the day before and decided a drink with a sandwich in his room would be preferable to the formality of lunch. Taking Captain Brown's diary with him he took up a comfortable position on the lounger on his balcony and opened the brown leather-covered little book. Two hours later he woke up, the book open on the second page. Feeling refreshed he now got down to reading it. As Rhoda predicted he would have found it dull had it not been for the personal interest with which he read it. He was intrigued to find the theme of hidden treasure cropping up again. But the emerald which had been involved in Rhoda's adventure in Switzerland was real. Here was the illusory idea of getting rich quick of a weak if imaginative character. Unable to escape from the reality of his father's domination, Alexander Seaton had taken refuge in fantasy. Napoleon's captors made sure the raw material of war – money – was not available in his final exile. The pathetic gift of his bust left for his favourite sister was evidence of this. Her affection for him had been an expensive luxury on Elba and was not likely to bring her to the dreary life on St Helena even if it had been permitted. Could he have hoped that, turned back at Madeira, she would take the statue as a message that Napoleon was still emperor in mind and she should rally his supporters? No, he was indulging in fantasy. Even the diamond necklace that Pauline had returned to him before Waterloo was accounted for – loot to the Huns though the theft was never acknowledged.

Lost treasure did not take the form of easily portable objects nowadays. Spanish galleons yielding loads of doubloons belonged to the old *Boys' Own* tradition. Modern technology now pinpointed the sites of sunken trading vessels and treasure hunters paid taxes on their finds. Still, young Seaton had been a boy in the heyday of the *Boys' Own*. His wretched childhood spent in England, separated from his parents in India, would have encouraged escapist fantasies to make life bearable. Davenport felt a twinge of pity for Alexander

Seaton, then laughed at himself. Young Seaton had long become old Seaton and was dead. Pity was best expended on those still living and there to be helped as Rhoda had tried to help Olga Bayne. Was that the cause of the nasty trick she had played on Rhoda? It is more blessed to give than to receive but those on the receiving end usually feel bitter resentment against their fate. Davenport intended to meet Olga Bayne as soon as possible and judge her capacity for spite. He knew he would have to wait for Rhoda's return for that but he thought he could manage a meeting with Mrs de Lisle and Miss Putley on the grounds of their common acquaintance. He had gathered from Rhoda that they usually had a drink at the bar of her hotel before dinner and from her description of them he thought they would be easily identifiable especially if they were together.

That evening proved his anticipation was justified. He arrived at the bar to hear the words, 'A dry sherry please. Very dry.' He walked up to the speaker and said,

'I think you must be Mrs de Lisle. Rhoda Brown mentioned you. I'm Matthew Davenport.'

Mrs de Lisle looked somewhat taken aback at being addressed by a stranger but Davenport's old school tie and gentlemanly appearance prejudiced her in his favour before her mind registered Rhoda's introduction.

'Good evening. I hope Miss Brown is fully recovered.'

'Yes. She is ready to return here tomorrow thanks partly to your kindness I believe.'

'I'm glad we were able to help. Let me introduce my friend, Miss Putley.'

They exchanged an amused twinkle with the conventional greeting. Mrs de Lisle's grande dame manner, though natural to her, came over almost as a parody to him and and he saw Miss Putley realised this without thinking any the less of her friend. He appreciated the loyalty.

'I hope you will give me the pleasure of dining with me?'

Pixie looked delighted and Constance, though feeling Davenport was advancing rather quickly, was only too aware of the shortage of single men of personable appearance in her age group and accepted the invitation graciously.

They moved on to the dining-room where Davenport intended to hear a full account of Rhoda's mishap from two observers. He knew he would have to get thoroughly established in the good graces of the two very different ladies before they would be willing to talk about her so it was not until they were settled with coffee and liqueurs that he spoke of Rhoda again.

Pixie gave him an opening by asking if he had known Rhoda long.

'Not very long but we happened to be staying in the same guest house in Alpenwold and discovered that Rhoda's father had known a great-uncle of mine whom he met in the same area of Switzerland. You may have read in the papers about the discovery of an emerald which was sold for the benefit of the Church.'

'Were you involved in that?'

Neither Constance nor Pixie was immune to the thrill of knowing someone on the inside of a good story with no scandalous overtones – so rare an occurrence that it must give exceptional delight as it could be repeated indefinitely at home without injuring anyone's reputation. Davenport decided it was worth acquiring a sympathetic audience and gave them the outlines of the story of the recovery of the Spanish *Imperial Emerald*. Both listeners were fascinated and Davenport decided to follow up immediately with their version of Rhoda's unpleasant experience as it would save Rhoda from having to refer to it unnecessarily. Neither, however, was able to add much to the outline she had given them. They knew now that Olga Bayne had administered the banned ointment.

'A very undesirable acquaintance,' Constance said firmly.

'They met in the church garden,' Pixie reminded her.

'The church is altogether too comprehensive nowadays. When we were young that type of person went to chapel.'

Davenport was moved to wonder whether, as a result, St Peter had found difficulty in filling the Anglican corner of Paradise. Perhaps in his blundering way he had got over his vision of the clean and unclean creatures by authorising gentiles in the church only in the overseas branches. Knowing that Constance would be bewildered by such a train of thought and even Pixie would find it inappropriate to discuss theology over liqueurs, he asked if they were acquainted themselves with Olga Bayne.

'Indeed no.'

'I had a few words with her after she called on Rhoda to return the ointment for the doctor. I met her coming out of the lift when

I was going up and she looked so miserable I stopped for a few words.' Needless to say this was from Pixie.

'Was Rhoda so ill then?'

'No, she was much better but of course Miss Bayne must have felt responsible. I suppose she had been in possession of an illegal drug and may have been afraid of police repercussions.'

'It was reported to the police then?'

'Not officially. No forms were filled in as Rhoda did not want to claim for insurance. The doctor must have notified the police but only verbally as Rhoda was very decided about them not being involved.'

'I can't think why,' said Constance. 'I should have thought she would have felt it her duty to have that young woman at least reprimanded.'

Neither of her auditors took this up. Davenport knew well why Rhoda would not want an interview with the police. The approach of the Swiss inspector who treated her story as the fantasy of a woman of a 'certain age' had so infuriated her that she was unlikely to lay herself open to another such interview.

The ladies, now realising it was getting late, rose and exchanged thanks for a delightful evening, looking forward to a repetition after Rhoda's return. As Rhoda had foretold, Davenport had enjoyed meeting Constance and Pixie. To him they were a refreshing change from the intellectual feminists he often met in Oxford. He enjoyed having his company appreciated just because he was a man, an experience which not even Rhoda accorded. Pleased with himself and his surroundings he strolled back to Reid's.

Next day he rang up Rhoda after giving her time to settle back in her hotel and suggested they should share a tourist lunch on the Beatles' boat. There would be sufficient breeze on the front to be agreeable as it was a hot day and swimming was out for her. She was pleased to fall in with his plans and together they ambled through St Catherine's park, with the scent of the flowers around them and a view of a cruise ship in the harbour. No conversation was necessary. They had reached the stage of friendship when it was unnecessary to fill silences. They were unconscious of the envious or admiring glances of which they were a target for they were a handsome and distinguished-looking couple.

Arrived at the Beatles' restaurant, they agreed that the luxuries of successful pop stars were not always wasted. The spaciously set out tables and the proximity of the water made for a restful time that both appreciated. It was mid afternoon before they bestirred themselves to go back to their hotels. Davenport had told Rhoda of his contrived meeting with Pixie and Constance and she promised to arrange that they should expect him for dinner again.

Meanwhile, having spotted the Roscommon children in the paddling pool, Rhoda went to enjoy the company of those for whom personal adult gossip had no interest. They greeted her politely and returned to their occupation of splashing one another impartially. Bea had evidently forgotten her royal dignity and finding she was getting the worst of the game scrambled out to join Rhoda. She greeted her again affectionately leaving large, damp patches on Rhoda's dress.

'Napoleon's been smashed,' she confided.

Rhoda was at a loss. Was the splashing a re-enactment of the battle of the Nile or was Napoleon the name for a toy that had gone the way of all toys (except those cherished by parents as long term investments – a fate not likely to overcome the chaplain's children's possessions).

Mark and John emerged from the pool.

'Shut up, Bea.'

'Shut up yourself,' retorted Bea.

'Daddy told us not to talk about it.'

'Ooh, so he did. I forgot.'

John turned to Rhoda with as much dignity as a boy of seven in brief bathing trunks could assume and said.'

'It is a matter concerning the church' – a phrase they were familiar with as a warning to little pitchers.

'Then I'll forget it too,' said Rhoda obligingly and the boys returned to the pool thankfully leaving their small sister to be looked after by someone else who was to be trusted with her indiscretions.

'I'd like to lie on your lounger. We're not allowed to go on them by ourselves.'

'You may certainly have mine. I'll try another.'

Rhoda settled herself in comfort while Bea bounced around enjoying the forbidden pleasure to the full. Rhoda would have liked to suggest an ice cream to secure a few minutes' peace but guessed that also was forbidden. Fortunately before she was faced with the

101

problem of paying tactfully for a damaged chair, Olivia Roscommon appeared.

'Five more minutes in the pool,' she said to her daughter, heaving her off the chair and taking it herself. Assured that the parental eye would secure fair play, Bea returned happily to the pool, managing to slosh a good splash into the boys' faces before they were aware of her return.

'You look tired,' Rhoda said sympathetically to Olivia.

'I am,' she replied. 'We had a break in at the church last night and it is very upsetting for Barnabas. Not having a church building in our last parish we tended to forget what a central place it has in the life of a parish and how much it is cherished for its own sake. Barnabas has been involved all day with churchwardens, police and what have you.'

'Was much damage done?'

'No. That's what is so worrying. We're used to dealing with vandals but here breaking in to a consecrated building is still regarded as sacrilege. After all it is open during the day so why on earth should anyone break in? But whoever it was knocked over that statue of Napoleon and broke it to pieces. It was a worthless thing but of course it had historic interest.'

'Could it have been done by a cat?'

'It could but if so it was done the same night as the padlock of the gates was forced. That was the only other evidence of the break in. We heard nothing so it must have all been done very quietly since the neighbourhood dogs didn't raise an unusual racket.'

'The dog that didn't bark in the night in the manner of a Sherlock Holmes story?'

'Oh, they barked but we have got so accustomed to them after six months here that we only notice if a pack of strays start a noisy fight in the street.'

'Well the statue had no sacred significance,' Rhoda said consolingly.

'No, but like Lady Macbeth, I would have preferred it not to have happened in *our* chaplaincy. Fusses over non-essentials irritate Barnabas so and though his mind recognises they can be important to other people, his nerves won't. He was getting better too.'

'Can't he leave it to the churchwardens? After all, if it were an interregnum they would have to cope and they must be more familiar with police on the island than your husband.'

'I'm sure they will manage everything in the end but he can't refrain from taking the weight of the world on his shoulders to begin with.'

Though there was a note of exasperation in Olivia's voice, she managed to laugh at herself and calling the children out of the pool, she got them dried and dressed with such nannie assistance as Rhoda, unfamiliar with the society of small children, was able to contribute.

'Thanks for listening to my moan. I shall be so bored with it all as it's bound to be the topic of conversation for the next week.'

'Have a day away from it,' said Rhoda whose fellow feeling moved her to suggest rashly that Olivia and the children should join her on an expedition the next day. 'We'll go to that park in the hills and they can run riot while you have a rest. I'll get one or two friends to join us and we can take turns in keeping an eye on the children. There's a good restaurant where we can have a meal out of doors – they'll like that.'

This to those knowing Rhoda's dislike of picnics was a noble offer though mitigated by the fact they would at least have good food and wine not the ghastly burnt offerings of barbecues.

'That's very kind of you. The children would love it and I would like to get away. If Barnabas can manage without me I'd love to come.'

Barnabas appeared providentially to pick up his family. He appreciated the gift of the hotel in providing a rendezvous. It was of more value than money to him. Rhoda decided to use some kindly intentioned blackmail by asking Barnabas herself about lending his family for the expedition. Far from objecting he looked relieved.

'I'll go over to Machico to see my RC colleague about the ecumenical service and with none of us around to satisfy curiosity the curious will lose interest in the affair. I suppose Olivia told you about the broken statue?'

Rhoda, seeing the children had wandered out of earshot, told them of Bea's bewildering indiscretion and the prompt action of the boys to suppress her. Barnabas laughed.

'She's a bit young to be able to keep anything quiet. So are the boys but it is essential that a clerical family should never be thought to be a source of gossip.'

'More essential than the seal of the confessional,' suggested

Rhoda. 'Less likely to happen now that clerical visiting is reduced. Gossiping curates must have been a menace in the days when they had to visit every afternoon and there was always someone at home.'

'A curate of any sort would be a help nowadays. He wouldn't have time to gossip.' Barnabas spoke grimly from his own experience of overwork.

Just then the children rushed up having discovered a beetle in the grass which they wanted their father to identify. He moved off with them while Rhoda hastily arranged to pick them up at ten o'clock next morning.

She decided to ask Pixie and Constance to come with them as well as Matthew. Pixie, whose large heartedness was extended particularly to small children, would be a great help. Constance was safe among her own class and Matthew would ensure the pleasant coalition of the whole party. All she needed to do was to get hold of two reliable taxi drivers. It would not matter if their English was suspect as Olivia was a linguist and in her six months on the island had picked up enough Portuguese to do all necessary interpretation.

Davenport appeared at the bar of Rhoda's hotel before dinner and without formality took over getting the drinks. When they had sat together to enjoy them Rhoda issued her invitation for the morrow, explaining the shortness of notice. There was no need. The others had heard rumours about the break in, in a form varying from an attack on the chaplain to the theft of the alms boxes. Rhoda was able to inform them of the true amount of destruction and though Davenport looked at her sharply at the mention of the broken statue of Napoleon he said nothing of his thought at the moment. The coincidence of the break in of the church described in Captain Brown's diary must keep till they were alone.

The next day was one of Madeira's brightest, the sort that earned the island's title of paradise. Two taxis conveyed Mrs Roscommon and the children, Pixie and Constance, Rhoda and Davenport to the hills where the fresh breeze was welcome. Pixie had elected to share a taxi with the children and by the time they reached their destination they were firm friends. Pixie's long experience with Cubs and Brownies supplied her with a never-ending fund of activities for indoors or out, small or large places. The children tumbled out of their taxi bubbling over with their enjoyment of the taxi as the driver raised no objection to their playing a mouth organ and singing at intervals. They all talked at once in order to give their mother a comprehensive account of their activities. They would certainly want a repeat performance on the return journey. Fortunately Pixie's nerves were sound; she was not so sure of the road.

When she confided this to Rhoda, she recalled a favourite story of one of the guides for coaches, all driven by 'the best driver in the world'. A coach driver and a priest arrived together at the gates of heaven. When the coach driver stated his earthly occupation he was immediately admitted. The priest, however, was delayed and demanded to know the reason. His vocation should ensure admittance if the coach driver got in. 'Well,' said the hesitant doorkeeper, 'when you preached only two or three listened. When the coach driver was driving every passenger prayed.'

Pixie had very little time for conversation that day except over lunch when the children had their own small table and the adults had a good meal. Rhoda enjoyed the conversation more than the meal. Like Mr Woodhouse in Jane Austen's *Emma* who 'to have any of them sitting down out of doors to eat would inevitably make him ill', Rhoda saw no reason for picnics if a good dining-room was available. This compromise of proper chairs and a table of the right height made the outdoor consumption bearable if not enjoyable. For the children it was a delight. What food they were permitted was placed on their table to be eaten in what order they liked. The plastic tablecloth could not be injured by falling debris and their clothes were not the source of misery to them that they were to children of Rhoda's time. The washing machine enabled parents to observe the healthy precept that children should be clean only twice a day on getting up and on going to bed.

All except Olivia joined in their entertainment during the day. Rhoda could be only an assistant as she had no talent for amusing young children. Davenport was invaluable in all ball games ensuring that Bea did not fall behind her brothers in success but rather unfairly outstripping them. Even Constance showed an unexpected talent for story telling which came in later in the afternoon before Bea fell suddenly to sleep, indicating it was time to think of going home.

When Bea woke they assembled the playthings and went back as they came. Pixie told Rhoda afterwards that she had been able to enjoy the mouth organ herself as the children pressed it on her so that they could sing unimpeded. The driver was invited to join in and delighted them by interspersing the occasional chorus in Portuguese. It was nearing dinner time when they got back to Rhoda's hotel where Davenport elected to walk up to Reid's and Olivia took Pixie's place with the children. An excited medley of thanks from them and a more restrained but no less sincere repetition from their mother, and the taxi departed, the children waving wildly.

'Those children are very well behaved,' said Constance. She had been chiefly aware of them as they gazed with the angelic countenances, only seen normally when they were asleep, as she had told stories.

Pixie grinned sympathetically.

'You need a good night's rest,' she said. 'Anyway it was a good day for Olivia.'

Chapter 12

A Blind Journey

Davenport and Rhoda had arranged at the picnic to have the next day together. When he rang up it was to suggest that they should visit a garden combining holiday enjoyment with the opportunity to talk at leisure. He arrived an hour later in a taxi. Davenport had decided on Ribeiro Frio as a suitable destination for the day as the garden could be combined with a short *levada* walk later, if they still felt energetic. After a selective approach to the wealth of the garden they found a comfortable seat where they could talk without interruption.

'Well, coincidences are of more common occurrence than most people think,' began Rhoda.

'Yes. The really interesting point is that this break in of the church is the only one that has happened since that mentioned in your father's diary.'

'Can you be sure of that?'

'Pretty sure. I met someone at Reid's whose family is English Madeiran and he was sure he would have heard about it if it had happened. He was worried about it. Since the end of the dictatorship and the Revolution (more peaceful by the way even than its English equivalent in 1688), a lot of young people have been going to university on the mainland. He is afraid they may have been infected with permissive ideas that will lead to trouble. Up till now Madeira has escaped the worst features of affluent Western Europe in the way of crime and violence.'

'But you think it's a one-off incident associated with some expectation of finding a Napoleonic treasure?'

'I can't account otherwise for the break in at night. The church is open during the day and there is nothing to prevent anyone from going round at leisure.'

'If the statue was the objective why not put it in a shopping bag and carry it off?'

'It's absence might have been noticed almost immediately and suspicion would fall on the culprit. There's always someone around and weekday visitors are not so numerous that the thief would get away unsuspected. If the hypothetical treasure was in the statue it could only be broken unobserved at night.'

'So if there was anything the thief has now got away with it?'

'Yes, if he's here as a tourist he can walk through the green channel at Customs.'

'Risky. I've noticed young men are often the ones stopped in the random search. Besides why assume it was a man? The thief may have been a woman.'

'Or there may be two involved, man and woman?'

'You are thinking of the two involved in the mystery of the exchanged briefcases?'

'What a good title for a Sherlock Holmes story. I'm sure whoever broke the statue was inspired by the Holmes story.'

'Or by a disgusted art lover. The grand duchess's products were neither distinguished nor rare. To return to our muttons, could the briefcase pair be possible suspects? If the briefcases are interchangeable I suppose they could be used in some sleight of hand dodge but what would successful business people be engaged on a shady deal like that for? They looked very affluent.'

'Business people often do until they go bankrupt or get involved with the fraud squad. I wonder if they are still on the island. We might get to know them.'

'I had only that brief glimpse and that was before I went to Machico. They wouldn't linger if they had been involved in a theft.'

'It's not always easy to get a flight when you want it – besides it is fatal to change plans suddenly. It provokes suspicion unnecessarily.'

'And of course since it's extremely improbable there was anything in the statue or that there was ever a Napoleonic treasure to begin with we are wasting our time in these blind alleys.'

'Oh no. Not wasting time. All these speculations are entertaining.'

'But the incident was not entertaining for the poor Roscommons.'

'No, and if there is any foundation for the belief in a lost treasure and nothing was found in the statue we have the unpleasant fact that there is a burglar at large who may attack elsewhere. There was an unpleasant implication of violence. The statue appeared to have been jumped on and smashed to smithereens.'

'So all we have to do is find the thief's boots and examine them for marble dust.'

'Let's have a spell of flower-watching to revive our spirits.'

They wandered on, meeting no one they knew so there was nothing to distract their minds from the problem in hand: it was not surprising therefore that when they next spoke it was to voice the same thought.

'The diary.'

'Yes,' said Matthew. 'We must go through it carefully and also try to find out on what grounds Alexander Seaton came to have that obsession. He was a weak character but apparently not stupid so it is unlikely that it was entirely fantasy. We seem to light on these problems when I'm cut off from a library. Or better still in Oxford there is certain to be an authority on Napoleon's exile who could enlighten me on all the possibilities. His inertia on St Helena seems to have been due to illness and he may well have arrived there with every intention of staging a comeback so realistically he must have planned accessible resources.'

'Diamond necklaces wouldn't go far in financing a war.'

'No but they make handsome bribes in escaping imprisonment and once back in France he could hope for support again. After all Napoleon III got in partly on the strength of his name a generation after the emperor's death.'

'Well, speculation isn't enough; we must get evidence as the detectives of fiction are always saying.'

'Yes, the only fact we have so far is your mishap on the *levada* and even for that you are not sure that Olga Bayne pushed you.'

'No, and in any case I can't see her or her boyfriend as burglars. Financial cheating with the aid of computers possibly but not involved with personal violence.'

By mutual consent the topic was abandoned for the rest of the visit and a short but enjoyable *levada* walk completed their excursion. Rhoda suggested tea in her room as providing a suitable opportunity for examining the diary in the light of the phenomenal break in of the church and after tea they took the brown leather volume out on the balcony and read it aloud, each taking an entry. Both found interest in the record of the unchanging aspects in Madeira but gave most attention to the entries relating to the break in of the church. They agreed that the explanation given by Captain Brown was probably the correct one. However low he sank, Alexander Seaton was unlikely to steal and he had already had ample opportunity to examine the bust at the chaplain's invitation.

'If anyone had read the diary with theft in mind it would account for breaking the statue as an external examination had been no use.'

'But no one has had access to it. As it is so small I have kept it locked in my bureau at home and it has been in my room here except when I lent it to you.'

'And I kept it in my pocket so it was never out of my possession till I returned it.'

'So we are left with an unexplained accident and a burglarious coincidence as the only facts relating you to the affair. It is rather a tenuous connection.'

'Not to mention the fact that the accident was not serious except to my reputation for sobriety and the burglary resulted in nothing but the loss of a mass-produced statue.' In Matthew's presence, Rhoda was now able to laugh at her misadventure and he felt his unexpected visit to Madeira had been worthwhile, both in bringing her consolation and the diversion of a minor mystery.

Davenport suggested she should come to dinner at Reid's with him but she declined on the excuse of fatigue though, in fact, her reason was that she was not yet ready to get on the horse from which she had fallen and would prefer delaying her return to Reid's when there would be less chance of her being recognised as the protagonist in a conspicuous scene. So they said *Au revoir* and Davenport went back alone to his hotel where he hoped for another encounter with the English Madeiran from whom he might get further information on the background of Seaton's associations with Napoleon's visit.

In this he was disappointed and decided that until he met Olga Bayne and her Alec, further speculation was useless. The next day he asked Rhoda if she could arrange a meeting.

'I doubt it. I don't even know if Olga is still on the island. I gather she was spending her savings on the holiday. Moreover she did not seem at all keen that I should get to know her Alec. When we met she all but interrupted me mid sentence to get him away.'

'Odd. In the Noah's-Ark society of the present day I should have thought she would be glad to show she had a presentable partner. You said he was good looking.'

'Yes, very attractive in the manner of the young. Some years younger than Olga I would say.'

'Perhaps that was the trouble. She didn't want you to think she was cradle snatching.'

'Oh no, the difference was not great enough for that. I think it was just her natural ungracious manner. If she had left the island that would prove she has no connection with the treasure hunt.'

'Or that she had succeeded and departed with the booty. You say she was staying at a hotel in the centre. Let's go down and try one or two for coffee and I'll enquire if she's staying there.'

'Won't she think it odd if we run into her?'

'Why should she? You could reassure her that there would be no trouble about her possession of the ointment and show you feel no ill-will towards her. She might be glad to know you have no ill effects if she was innocent of malign intentions.'

'Yes, I should like to see her again. In spite of her off-putting manner I think I could get to like her. She had a latent sense of humour.'

'Shall we walk down or take a taxi?'

'Walk. We can take a taxi back.'

So they set off through the park to the city centre. There were several hotels near the cathedral, encircled like all cathedrals with scaffolding, and Rhoda shuddered as she saw a young man negotiating his way on such frail support.

'Cold?' asked Matthew.

'No. Just look at that youth.'

'He's all right. They've used that sort of scaffolding for centuries. They built medieval cathedrals without modern equipment.'

'And what was the casualty rate?'

'Probably less than now. They weren't in such a hurry.'

They paused as a stream of traffic shot past underlining Davenport's point. In the narrow streets further confined by parked cars they had to walk in single file and Rhoda began to regret having embarked on this expedition. However a small but attractive foyer

111

emerged within sight as she pressed between its window and a parked car.

'With bar,' she said thankfully and escaped within.

Davenport arrived at her side after some delay owing to his adherence to the custom of 'women and children first'. Two girls and a woman with a pushchair took some time to edge through the constricted space available to pedestrians.

Rhoda had taken a seat but no waiter appeared until Davenport sat beside her. She was reminded of an incident on another occasion when she had taken a seat alone at a restaurant and was asked by a young waiter, 'Where is your husband?'

Annoyed at the assumption that a single was negligible, Rhoda snapped,

'Tea for ONE.'

Feeling compunction she resorted to fiction, gabbling something about a widow travelling alone, ending,

'I am seventy'.

Recognising only the number the boy commented solemnly,

'That is very old.'

She told Davenport the story and he laughed as Rhoda had intended but she was not altogether sure she was amused herself. Having led a very quiet life in the last years of the life of her mother, who died at the age of ninety-four, she found the discrimination against single women very irritating and only her sense of humour saved her from the extremes of feminism. What must it have been like for the Mrs Pankhursts if this represented nearly a century's progress?

Having ordered coffee, Matthew had gone to the reception desk to enquire if Miss Bayne was staying there. He was told that she was but there was no reply when the receptionist rang through to her room.

'Do you wish to leave a message?'

'Perhaps when we leave, if she has not returned by then.' Davenport returned to the table.

'We've struck lucky first time. Miss Bayne is staying here though she is out just now. Just as well as we'd better decide on our next step first. Shall we invite her and the young man to dinner?'

'I think that might strike Olga as suspiciously lavish. Let's wait to see if she comes in while we're here and then it would be natural to ask her to have a drink with us.'

Davenport agreed. Pleasantly cut off from the whirl of life outside, they were able to enjoy watching it at close quarters without the whirling breezes encountered in the street cafés. As at Machico, there was plenty of student life, contrasting with business encounters and, as always, the skill of drivers negotiating their way round parked vehicles. They spent half an hour companionably with the occasional desultory remark when Rhoda caught sight of Olga coming up the street.

'Don't look now. Olga is in sight. I'm going to bend down and fasten my shoe in case she decides to dodge.'

When Olga was safely inside the door Rhoda got up and it was clear from the other's expression that she would have avoided her had it been possible. Rhoda gave her no opportunity. She went towards her with her hand held out,

'How nice to run into you. Won't you join us for a drink?'

Olga was obviously unable to think of a reason why not but she did say that she musn't stay long as she was going out again. Rhoda introduced Davenport who tided over an ungracious reception by asking her what she would have and departed to the bar leaving Rhoda to pick up the threads of their acquaintanceship. Olga took the lead by asking after Rhoda's leg and when assured there were no complications looked relieved but still far from pleased at the meeting. Rhoda plunged in as Davenport brought the drinks.

'Is your friend still here?'

'Yes,' said Olga bluntly, leaving the others to promote conversation.

'Shall we see you at the church this Sunday?' Rhoda tried again.

'No.'

Rhoda gave up and Davenport took the strain, asking about the hotel and chatting about the tourist amenities. Olga showed little interest but Davenport had not entertained tongue-tied students for nothing. He kept going until Olga relaxed her guard and even made the occasional comment herself. Rhoda breathed a sigh of relief.

'Will you have time to come to tea with me again?' she asked.

Olga hesitated.

'And bring your friend. Mr Davenport will keep him in countenance if he finds one lady dull.'

'Shall I ring you when I find out if he's free?'

'Yes. Do that. Today or Monday will be all right.'

Rhoda was about to get to her feet when Davenport added, 'Have you heard about the break in at the church?'

Olga sat quite still for a moment and then said, 'No. What happened?'

Taking her cue from Davenport, Rhoda told her of the smashed bust of Napoleon.

'Sounds like the Sherlock Holmes story,' she said. 'Sorry I must go now or I'll be late. I'll give you a ring after lunch. Thanks for the drink.'

Almost before Davenport had got to his feet, she was half way up the stairs.

'Did we strike a chord?' asked Matthew as they got to a pavement wide enough for conversation.

'I think we did. But what chord I don't know. She is so ready to take offence that she might have thought you associated her with the shady dealings, that I had told you about her dismissal over the misuse of the computer at her office.'

'Well, we must wait to see if they take up your invitation.'

They went back to Rhoda's hotel and had lunch. They decided to wait for an hour to see if Olga would ring before they separated for the afternoon. If she accepted their invitation Davenport would come back to tea. Olga did ring but said Alec was unable to come and made it clear she would prefer to see Rhoda alone. As the next day was Sunday, Davenport arranged to walk to church with Rhoda when she could tell him if anything of interest had come out of Olga's visit.

Olga arrived in a hard mood. Rhoda wondered if she had quarrelled with Alec as she did not mention him and Rhoda was of the generation that could not ask intrusive personal questions.

'If your leg all right?' Olga asked abruptly.

Rhoda showed her the healed scar around which the bruising had gone.

'Oh good.'

Olga relapsed into her usual silence leaving Rhoda trying to think of something to say which would not offend. Fortunately tea arrived at that point and in the bustle of settling the tray and signing the bill the embarrassing silence could be broken by recalling how Olga liked her tea and whether she took sugar. Rhoda went on to talk about her stay in Machico and how much she had enjoyed the change of scene.

114

The atmosphere having become less tense, Olga volunteered a remark. Having no prejudice against intrusive personal questions she asked bluntly,

'Who is Mr Davenport?'

'He is a friend,' replied Rhoda rather coldly. Seeing this was not going to satisfy Olga she added, 'He was an Oxford don. He retired recently.' Then thinking she might make an opening for Davenport to meet Olga, 'If you did think seriously of taking a degree he might be able to help you with advice.'

'I'm not likely to take an Oxford degree. It would have to be Open University or a polytechnic where I could keep a job going.'

'If he got to know you, he could be a referee.'

Olga looked thoughtful. One of the disadvantages in being poor was the trap that you never got to know anyone influential and without knowing someone influential you never had a chance of the best jobs. You had to be so much better than others that they *had* to put you on the shortlist. Why cut off her nose to spite her face? Here was a chance to get to know someone who, like Rhoda, was not only rich but, unlike her, had a wide experience in the working world. Whatever her prejudices, Olga had enough sense to know that anyone in education was very much part of the working or more likely the overworking world. Moreover most of them earned so little in relation to their ability and qualifications that they did not lose touch with reality and usually had sufficient imagination to realise the problems of a woman of her background. Davenport must be rich or he wouldn't be staying at Reid's but he had still struck her as a sympathetic personality.

'I should like to meet him,' she said awkwardly for she knew she could not have made a good impression on him at their morning meeting.

'Are you going to church tomorrow?'

Olga hesitated. Then making up her mind that whatever the mental obstacle which held her back she was not going to miss this chance,

'Yes, I shall be there.'

'Good, then you will meet him after the service. We are going together.'

Olga seemed relieved that the meeting would be an informal one and in a situation where she could easily escape if any awkward questions arose. She actually smiled at Rhoda who wished she

115

would do it more often for her face lightened to such an attractive expression that she was almost handsome. Rhoda smiled back. They were able to talk more freely than before. She gave an account of the picnic for the Roscommon children and Olga told some quite amusing stories of her experiences of life in a bedsit, sardonically but without bitterness. They parted amicably, Olga having the talent 'to withdraw her foot from the neighbour's house' in good time, a talent which Rhoda had not always observed among her supposedly well bred friends.

After she had gone she rang up Matthew to let him know to what she had committed him.

'I'll do my best,' he promised, 'but on the surface the material isn't too attractive.'

Rhoda had to admit to herself that this was true. Yet she could not help a feeling of friendliness towards Olga as she felt to the other acquaintances of this holiday. She had none of the attraction that good manners gave the Grantleys and the Heathcotes or sheer human contrast to Constance and Pixie. Certainly Olga could attract none of the admiration she felt for the Roscommons. Yet in a way Rhoda found her as interesting as Martha Wood and decided that it was probably their independent personalities that she liked. She did not want people to lean on her; she felt no need to be needed. Neither of them needed her though it was pleasant to think she might be useful to Olga.

As for the unfortunate results of her accident she was now convinced that Olga had had no intention of harming her. It would have been a pointless piece of malice and with all her faults Olga did not appear to be malicious. If she were, she would not allow herself to be exploited by a drop-out like Alec. Yet when she came to think of it she had no evidence that Alec did exploit Olga. On the contrary he might be the only one bringing some human affection into her life. It was the prejudice resulting from his being younger that had produced the thought. Much wider disparities of age had resulted in happy marriages – such as Doctor Johnson's and Disraeli's. Probably the source of the prejudice like so much else went back to Shakespeare and the second-best bed he left his wife, probably because she liked it better than the other. What a lot of sheer boring repetitiveness there was in the world of biography. Every detail had to be exploited in order to produce something new in endless books on the same person, when the past and present were full of personalities whom no one wrote about because publishers wanted the ready-made advertisement of a famous or infamous name.

Rhoda realised her thoughts had wandered far from Olga. Looking at her bedside table she saw her father's diary and suddenly remembered the day when it had disappeared from sight for a few hours. It was the day she had spent in her room after the accident when Olga had visited her twice. She recalled how odd her manner had been. She put it down to her feeling of responsibility for Rhoda's troubles. Was it possible that instead she had taken the opportunity to abstract the diary that day, read it and return it later when she brought back the banned ointment? Rhoda had been in no condition to observe closely what her visitors were doing at the time. She shook her head. Really her adventure in Switzerland had resulted in an over-stimulated imagination. The Napoleonic treasure had never existed. His enemies had been careful to ensure his final exile was no second Elba. It was a matter of historic record that he had been deprived of all resources before he got to St Helena.

She picked up a book and went to her balcony. She did not open the paperback because the view distracted her. The rose and gold sunset in the evening flow of clouds over Reid's was more attractive than any romantic story. It was the stuff that poetry is made of:

> A voiceless, dreamless paradise
> Of fleeing and fantastic form
> More lovely than the fierce sunrise,
> More visionary than the storm.

Chapter 13

Island in Blue of Summer

Rhoda woke up next day with a feeling of well-being that comes sometimes without any particular cause to a person who is fit and has a free day ahead. With conscious thought she realised it was Sunday, a day for her of pleasant associations. She had no need of American-sized newspapers to pass her day. Church and hospitality had been the pattern of the first day of the week all her life. The breakfast solitude over coffee and rolls added to the conviction that this was to be a halcyon day. It was partly due to the fact that in the last years of her mother's life it was the only time she could be sure of being alone and she valued its continuance.

Matthew appeared in good time for a saunter to church. The day was fine and the glow of blossom and the blue of the sea combined in an aura of vivid colour. Rhoda felt as she often did in Madeira that they were back in an earlier era, more peaceable and exotic than the violent twentieth century with its advanced technology and depleted humanity. She told Matthew that her suspicions had vanished and that she had let her imagination, or her cocaine-induced hallucinations, run away with her. Davenport was not so sure. The break in of a church on Madeira was more sinister than it would be elsewhere but he saw no reason to associate it with Rhoda's misadventure and decided it was time to take tea at Reid's again.

'If we meet Mrs de Lisle and Miss Putley at church shall I invite them to join us for tea at Reid's today?'

Rhoda hesitated for only a moment.

'Yes, of course. I should like to make up to them for the catastrophe last time. Tea at Reid's is supposed to be such a civilised affair,' she added ruefully.

'That's one of the reasons I booked in at Reid's. I have been establishing a conventional reputation, correct dress, correct ties and a parody of the gentleman scholar that should impress any maître d'hotel with the desirability of any guest of mine.'

Rhoda smiled.

'I shall look forward to the occasion in your company,' she said sincerely.

They arrived in good time and strolled round the garden before going in to the service. The congregation as usual filled the nave and Rhoda wondered if it ever overflowed into the gallery. She saw familiar faces as they were seated towards the back of the church and was glad that Olga had come. It would be nice to know that her holiday had helped to get her restarted in a more congenial working life than she had known before. As the day was fine there was a large gathering in the garden after the service and Rhoda immediately steered Davenport to Olga and introduced them. Pixie and Constance were in a group but Rhoda could see them at any time and was delighted to see the Heathcotes in an accessible spot.

'Intelligent clergyman,' Agnes Heathcote wasted no time on conventional remarks about the weather.

'Yes, and a delightful family.' Rhoda used the term in a different sense from Mrs de Lisle when referring to the Roscommons.

'What are they doing here?' asked her husband who recognised in Barnabas Roscommon the sort of pastor who did not choose pleasant backwaters.

Rhoda told them what she knew of their background. Finding that this was the Heathcotes first visit to Funchal, she also invited them to lunch with her and Davenport but they were engaged to friends who were over in a time-share flat and had to be on their way.

Davenport came up at that moment and Rhoda looked round for Olga.

'She's gone. I think she was in a hurry to get back to her young man who is evidently no church goer.'

'What a pity. I was going to ask her to lunch so that you could see her in company but perhaps it's just as well. Constance would raise her hackles.'

'There they are. Let's go and ask them about tea.'

Pixie was delighted with the invitation partly because it showed Rhoda's complete recovery. Constance was less appreciative probably fearing recognition of the previous visit but she accepted graciously and they arranged to take a taxi together as, though the distance was small, it was uphill.

Just then three small figures appeared clutching plates of tit-bits which they pressed on Pixie, recognising her as the playmate of their day out. Pixie obligingly took something off each plate and urged the children to share the goodies with the others. The boys politely obeyed but Bea hung on firmly to Pixie's skirt and insisted they were all for her.

'And me,' Bea added.

'We get what's left over,' Mark and John explained leaving it to their better nature to refuse second helpings. All obliged and Davenport and Rhoda kindly removed the plates and handed the contents bit by bit to the boys.

'You'll spoil your lunch,' Constance warned severely but Mark and John knew better. Hors d'oeuvres had no effect on their appetites.

Meanwhile the Grantleys had come up and by diverting some of the plate's contents to them, Pixie saved Bea from indigestion without losing her good will.

Barnabas had now joined his wife and came up to collect the children and conversation became mixed. Bea had to be restrained from joining in but Mark and John, familiar with the situation, had withdrawn a puzzle from their pockets and were quietly engaged in seeing who could do it first. Davenport as usual found common acquaintances with Barnabas through the university and they continued chatting until they became aware that the crowd in the garden had dwindled and it was time to separate.

Rhoda, finding the Grantleys free, had asked them to have lunch with her and Davenport. She felt an obligation to those who had stood by her after the accident and knew Matthew liked company. He would be interested in Frank Grantley's inside knowledge of business dealings on the island. Rhoda was intrigued by Harriet's membership of the Brick-layers' Union even if her bricklaying was confined to domestic gardens. Never having been involved in the world of work herself, Rhoda found information about different aspects of it fascinating and, unlike most people, liked to hear

120

people talk shop even when it was not her shop. Her reactions were interesting to those talking to her for her viewpoint was unmarked by the natural prejudices of those whose spoke from inside knowledge.

They walked down to the Beatles' boat restaurant as providing the best of an indoor-outdoor setting.

'I've never eaten out so much in my life before,' said Harriet. 'Frank's job meant I had to do a lot of entertaining of business clients and associates and though I like cooking I got rather tired of the shop talk. Here the prospective clients entertain us and I'm enjoying the change.'

She smiled brightly at her husband as she spoke and Rhoda thought he looked less tired than when they had first met. Probably the thought that his wife was reconciled to life in Madeira had taken some of the strain out of life for him.

'It's pleasant to be engaged in business without the hustle of my former job. Redundancy hasn't meant financial disaster for me but nowadays you're in or out. Lose your job and your whole world disappears overnight. Nobody has time to speak to you if they meet you in the street and if you called in at the office you'd be asked if you had an appointment.'

Frank tried to laugh but it was clear he hadn't forgotten the trauma that had brought him to Madeira. Rhoda thought of the whole areas of society where his experience had been repeated. Mines, steel works, dockyards. Not only the jobs but whole institutions disappeared almost overnight. What did life hold for the survivors? At least in a shipwreck rescuers were at hand. No such support existed for the survivors of business disaster. The love of money was the cause and money was the only balm offered – a superficial ointment offered for a mortal disease.

Davenport meanwhile, by his interest in Grantley's activities on the island, had restored cheerfulness to the atmosphere which lasted throughout the meal.

'We've met a lot of nice people here,' said Harriet as they thanked Davenport. 'I think we'll settle happily here. After all, it's in Europe if not in England.'

A siesta at their hotels beckoned Rhoda and Davenport and, taking a taxi up the hill, they parted to an old-fashioned Sunday afternoon dozing over books. Rhoda came to realising it was time to get ready for tea at Reid's and that special attention must be paid to outward appearances. A different dress from last time was essential, combining restraint with an air of affluence. Perhaps she ought to have arranged for a different hairstyle but since it fell into graceful waves if she washed it herself in soap and cold water, it would have been pointless. The finished result was an air of austere dignity which should be sufficient to differentiate her from her last appearance and she went down to the lobby well satisfied. The glance of approval from Constance and Pixie's involuntary exclamation of praise bolstered her morale still more and they got into their taxi in pleasurable anticipation.

Davenport awaited them as if for a chancellor of a university and they moved towards the terrace. But the OC Teas was not to be deceived. His memory for faces was not to be confused by outward elegance and he moved forward to intercept them and assure them tables for tea were fully booked. His mouth was open to speak when Davenport stepped up beside Constance who naturally led the way.

'My guests would like tea on the terrace,' he said haughtily.

Recognising an impeccable guest of the old school, the waiter adroitly changed his attitude to one of deference and led the way to the best table available. Rhoda seated herself with a sigh of relief exchanging an amused smile with Matthew in recognition of his dexterity in managing the little social drama. Constance and Pixie looked round on the scene with satisfaction. They thought no more of the previous disastrous visit and settled to enjoy their position as guests of a guest instead of tourists 'doing' an island attraction. One of the pleasures lay in identifying those who belonged from those who did not. The tourists were indifferent to the tea. They enjoyed the view, looking over the garden to the limitless sea. Here no yapping dogs were audible, voices were automatically lowered, traditional dress recalled the leisured age of upper classes who had spent so much time daily in donning and changing it.

'A very pleasant spot,' said Constance giving her accolade.

'Yes, jolly nice.' Pixie smiled gratefully at Davenport. This time she was really going to enjoy the visit.

Davenport, pleased to see that Rhoda too was at ease, exerted himself to ensure their continued delight. The head waiter hovered attentively. To Constance's satisfaction no lesser waiter came to their table. Rhoda wondered how much this was due to Davenport and how much to the maître's determination to be on hand if trouble arose again. Whatever the reason she felt that Pixie and Constance were getting full compensation for her previous inadvertently disgraceful behaviour, the more so when Davenport led them into the hotel garden, debarred to the visiting tourist coming only for tea.

There, free from the wandering gaze of those at other tables, Rhoda looked round appreciatively while Davenport gave the others the history of the hotel from the time of the original Reid, the Scots boy who more than a century before had left home to seek his fortune with five pounds in his pocket. They sat together looking out to sea and Rhoda told Constance and Pixie more about her father's visit, bringing out the unchanging attractions of the island. This completed Rhoda's rehabilitation in Constance's eyes and, though this was not necessary for Pixie, she was glad to be in sympathy with her friend.

Davenport accompanied them to their taxi, all embarrassment exorcised, their memories of Reid's now of unalloyed pleasure. Rhoda was pleased when, in the taxi, both spoke warmly of Matthew. She had reason to be grateful for the deep-seated kindness that was basic to his character and she was all the more glad to see it expended on her friends not just for her sake but because of his genuine interest in the variety of human nature. It removed the debt of gratitude that can be so destructive of friendship. At dinner together that evening she felt that she and Pixie and Constance had moved from acquaintances to friends. Constance's snobbery and Pixie's exuberance would no longer jar on her. As part of the personality of friends these characteristics were accepted as part of them.

The next day Rhoda awoke with a holiday feeling. There was nothing she *had* to do. Such personal relationships as she had acquired this vacation were quiescent and undemanding. She could have a morning to herself with a clear conscience. In fact that was what she intended to have – a morning in the solitude of her own quarters and lunch too. She had always found the term 'everlasting life' repellent, with its connotation of endless time. 'Eternal' life communicated a sense of quality not quantity and that quality of life she was conscious of this morning. This sensation came very seldom and only when she was alone but it compensated for many a tedious hour of chronological living.

Davenport had, with his natural kindness, arranged to meet Olga

123

Bayne in the town so that they could discuss the possibilities of her future at leisure, something the after-service social at the church could not provide. Having made the introduction, Rhoda had decided to keep in the background. He was more likely to get a response from Olga's prickly personality if they were alone. He and Rhoda planned to go to Camara de Lobos in the afternoon and he could enlighten her then on his success or failure.

'Emotion recollected in tranquility' was one of the constituents of Rhoda's morning. She thought of the *levada* walk before her accident. The soft air, the brilliant yellow of the acacias; the sunlight dappling through the trees promoting a stillness of the spirit. Her inherited fortune had enabled her to escape the worst forms of the violent activism of the West. A Christian environment had given her the tools of meditation even though the church seldom provided opportunities to practise their use without complete withdrawal from the demands of daily living. Perhaps this was inevitable in the materialism of the West. The pursuit of money was incompatible with the development of the spirit. Rhoda recalled one of her favourite stories of the Desert Fathers. Two fathers decided they should try to experience conflict as in the world. As such conflict was usually due to quarrels over property they put a book between them. One Father said, 'I want that.' 'In that case you had better have it,' said the other and the conflict ended before it started.

The morning passed with extraordinary rapidity. It was time to ring room service for lunch and it called her back to everyday realities. She was to take a taxi with her favourite driver and pick up Matthew at Reid's. He was ready and waiting and the short drive to Camara barely gave time for the driver's introduction to the fishing village, where enormous families survived in spite of the post Revolution efforts to change life for women. He referred inevitably to Churchill's painting activities there, a fact of little interest to Rhoda who judged books and paintings for their intrinsic value not for the notoriety of author or painter.

They did see one Dickensian scene just after alighting from the taxi. A small girl sat on the pavement with a smaller child asleep in her lap. She held out her hand but they passed on. They were both healthy-looking children but the old ways had not been wiped out as they had in England in the days of the Welfare State. Rhoda remembered the fifties when no tramp appeared on the roads and no drunken derelicts occupied bus shelters or benches in gardens in small cathedral cities.

They walked along to the harbour where fishing was still a livelihood not a tourist attraction and finding a seat watched the view of nature and humanity with equal interest. After a time Rhoda remembered Matthew's morning.

'How did you get on with Olga?'

'I don't think I got very far. I get the impression of a divided personality. Oh, not in the schizophrenic sense but divided between the possibility of using her talents and some other option holding her back.'

'Then you think she has talent?'

'Yes. She has intelligence and could probably take a good degree provided she really wanted to do it.'

'Is it resentment at not having the opportunity at the usual time which is holding her back?'

'The impression I got was it something in the present, as if her decision could be made only when some scheme on hand now was completed. Has she any idea of getting a job here?'

'She gave me the impression she had come just for a holiday but of course something may have come up while she was here. Did she mention Alec?'

'No, and I gave an opening. I asked if she had a friend in the same position as herself as it is an incentive if some one else is pursuing a similar objective.'

'What did she say?'

'She didn't answer. I think deliberately because instead she asked an irrelevant question.'

'I'm sure he is at the bottom of her indecision. You should have seen how her eyes lit up when I mentioned the possibility of a university course.'

'I think you may be right. We got as far as clarifying that she would like to take a degree in Environmental Studies and her computer training would be useful. Perhaps this Alec has some get-rich-quick scheme he wants her to join him in. The pursuit of money is very tempting to those who have never had it. They think once they have it they can fulfil their personalities but they don't realise that the means of acquiring money, especially quickly, will change their personalities.'

'St Paul hit the nail on the head there. The love of money is the

125

root of all evil.' Rhoda thought of the Desert Fathers who gave up the conflict for property before it started. That was really the only way to deal with temptation.

'So it's left in the air?'

'I gave her my address and telephone number and said she must call me if she thought I would be of any help.'

'That is kind of you. I hope she won't prove a nuisance.'

'I'm not afraid of that but I am afraid she is going to let a chance of a new life go. I can't help her if she doesn't want to be helped. She must be about thirty and isn't going to do anything she doesn't want to. And it's a bad age to get mixed up with a drop-out when she's fed up with her own job.'

'Well, you have done your best. I won't try to get in touch with her but if we meet I'll see if there is any prospect of her confiding the reason for her hesitation.'

They left the harbour and set off up the hill to get a wider view. When they returned to the front Davenport decided their exertions warranted a reviver in the shape of the local poncha. And in the bar in the centre they found the best sample of that brew either of them had so far encountered on the island. They agreed to a sense of guilt at consuming poncha instead of tea and acknowledged that this must be the concomitant of joy introduced by the Fall of Man. Rhoda considered if the reason why people took such pleasure in hearing of and spreading tales of disaster, whilst it was so difficult to arouse interest in positive achievements. Humanity loved misery because guilt was the companion of joy; the current obsession with war and overwork was due to the fear that happiness would bring vengeance in its train. Odd that its strength should be stronger in 'Christian' civilisation than in pagan.

The refreshment of the drink was greater than the feeling of guilt and they returned to the taxi ready for more exploration. The viewpoint at Cabo Girao was the next obvious port of call. On arrival charming children pressed flowers in their hands, naturally expecting a quid pro quo. Davenport was unable to resist having less rigid opinions on the weaknesses of human nature than Rhoda and he left smiling faces behind him as he joined Rhoda on the top of the cliff. Rhoda did not find it as interesting as many other views she had seen on the island. She felt it was noted only because it was the highest and she had an instinctive prejudice against superlatives. She associated them with the attractions of fairs – the

126

fattest woman, the smallest dwarf – for which she had no inclination. Size without intrinsic merit had no allure for her. It was the
reason that travel programmes with vast arrays of food revolted her.
She belonged to the 'small is beautiful' school and every increase
in size, number, and expensiveness in Britain had filled her with
foreboding. Matthew, sensing her lack of enthusiasm, suggested it
was time to return to the taxi if they were to get back in time for
dinner and they returned to their patient driver.

Just after they passed through Camara, Rhoda noticed a young
man walking ahead and thought he looked familiar.

'Stop! I believe that is Alec.'

The driver acted on the command drawing up just in front of the
man.

'You *are* Olga's friend, Alec?'

'Yes,' he said and an engaging smile lit his face.

'Are you going back to Funchal? Can we give you a lift?'

'Thank you. I didn't fancy the walk but I'm stony broke,' again the
charming smile. He had probably got through life on the strength of
it. Rhoda could see him in his pram attracting the admiration
of impressionable old ladies. She wondered why she was so severe
in her judgement; she *knew* nothing about him.

She introduced him to Davenport.

'Olga told me about you. Nice of you to give her some help.'

'Not at all. It's a pleasure to talk to an intelligent young woman.'

'Yes, she's intelligent.'

Rhoda sensed some restraint in the comment. Olga's would be
the dominating personality in this partnership. Perhaps he resented
this although she felt he would always be under the domination of
some woman. The fact that Olga was neither beautiful nor rich
should tell in his favour. Rhoda observed him as he and Davenport
chatted. He had an easy manner and spoke with a slight air of
deference to the older man and that softened her judgement of him.
Certainly on the surface he was a much more attractive person than
Olga. It must be feminist prejudice that made her take Olga's part
– or feeling for the underdog. Olga had none of his superficial
charm to ease her path through life.

Alec asked to be put down in the Lido area. Rhoda saw Matthew
handing him a note which Alec took with a smile as if he were
conferring a favour on the giver.

'It was only 500 escudos,' said Matthew deprecatingly.

Rhoda realised she must have been looking disapproving and laughed.

'You believe he really was penniless?'

'Not penniless, but the more he gets from others the less he'll need from Olga.'

'You think he is living on her earnings?' She was shocked as if Alec were a gigolo of her mother's generation.

'I don't think they look on it that way nowadays.'

Rhoda laughed at herself. Whatever else feminism had changed it would be a long time before men stopped considering they were conferring the favour in a partnership. The necessity to live in couples even without a marriage tie was still as strong as the old Victorian idea that a single woman had failed in life and not <u>chosen</u> single status. It was to the credit of the younger generation that the economic tie was not the dominant factor. She recognised the strength of old customs. She knew that in Matthew's company she got more deference than on her own. The hotel in Machico was her first experience as a single woman in real equality with couples and single men and she gave unstinted admiration to the manager who had achieved this miracle.

She herself was not immune to old-fashioned ideas. She accepted the fact that Matthew paid the taxi driver with a handsome tip to take her on to her hotel. She had lived too long in her mother's Edwardian ambience to change completely and could not imagine trying to press half a taxi fare into Matthew's hand. She might try it some time to see how tactfully he refused. Alec, she was sure, would accept the whole fare with a charming smile.

Chapter 14

Postern of Fate

Olga and Alec sat on a bench looking at a cruise ship in the harbour.

'You were keen enough on the scheme three months ago,' Alec said.

'I'd just been sacked and hadn't had time to think it through.'

'Well, you have now and there's still a chance. We would be on easy street for the rest of our lives if it came off.'

'And if it didn't?'

'We'd wriggle out of it somehow; might even get a reward.'

'I don't like it. I think I'd rather take a degree, get a better job . . .'

'And settle down to boring nonentity,' Alec interrupted.

'It's more than the majority of the human race have the chance of.'

'We can't alter life for the human race. Why not settle to take care of ourselves.'

'I suppose it's my church orphanage upbringing. We were conditioned to think of others. We couldn't get away from them.'

Alec looked at her curiously. He had drifted into a relationship with her in the same way he had drifted through all other aspects of his life. He didn't understand her and there were times when he didn't even like her but she had been at hand when he was down and out and he felt a certain obligation to stick to her rather than try to find a more malleable partner for his plan.

'I suppose you want to keep in with your new aristocratic friends,' he said cruelly.

'What if I do?' she answered fiercely, 'I owe them.'

'But we're not going to do them any harm.' As always he placated her when she turned on him. 'In fact we're not going to do anyone any harm.'

'What about the cocaine?'

'I keep telling you there's no need to feel guilty about that. She'd have been perfectly all right if she'd gone straight home as you tried to arrange. Don't keep on about it. Her friend Davenport has enough influence to have straightened it all out.'

'What do you know about Davenport?'

'I was going to tell you. I went over to Camara yesterday to meet a chap. All right! We weren't up to anything that's any of your business. I decided to walk back and your friends picked me up in their taxi.' He smiled reminiscently aware that on strangers his charm might work.

'Did you make a touch?' she asked suspiciously.

'No I didn't. I just said I was stony broke and he pushed a 500-escudo note in my hand as I got out of the taxi. He might have made it a thousand.'

Olga sighed impatiently. Her fierce independence made his easy reliance on others repellent to her. But when he smiled on her she melted. His type was new in her life. She had never been popular with men and the crude manners and cruder language of those she had encountered disgusted her. She had met Alec at a coffee bar when he saw an empty chair at her table. His smiling courtesy and cultured voice offered a welcome novelty in the ugly and cramped bedsitter life of a woman working in London. If he had been a total phoney she would have recognised the fact, enjoyed the half hour and seen him no more. But he wasn't. He had all the charm of a successful con man. He really liked meeting people. He liked all aspects of life except work for which he was totally unfitted. He was not strong enough physically or mentally to make his way in the rat race and he had never tried. A superficial musical ability combined with an excellent singing voice had enabled him to exist as a last-minute substitute on the edge of climbing pop groups of all types, but he never became a member and preferred to get a subsistence with a few hours' street singing. To do him justice success as acquired in the modern world of art or business had no appeal for him. In the third-rate private school at which he had been educated, he had read and written poetry and sung in the choir. He had barely an introduction to other badly taught subjects which a succession of poorly qualified and unmotivated masters had nominally provided. He had been the victim of his father's snobbery and had left the school as soon as the law of the land permitted and at the same time left home. His mother had died long before and, having at last realised he actively disliked his father, he took off to London. Since then his rootless existence had taken him to many parts of the world and the last few months, since he had met Olga, had been his most settled since he was sixteen. It was to her that he had first confided his memories of a kindly but ineffective grandfather whose dreams had probably been influential in alluring him from the harsh realities of life to his irresponsible way of existence. He was nine when the old man died and from that time there had been no real home for him, though his charm often resulted in his doing very well out of neighbours who disliked his father's pretensions of being a cut above them.

'Well, are you or aren't you coming in with me?'

'I'm already in,' she said bitterly. It was true no one else would be harmed and in sharing the enterprise with him there would not only be a way of escape from the dreary bedsit existence but there would be the hold which might lead to building up a permanent relationship between them. She was four years the elder, old enough for a rootless existence to have no attraction and Alec would be happy if he had the means to live comfortably. They might settle down in France or Portugal where civilised existence was more readily obtainable than in England.

'Yes, we'll go ahead as planned and if nothing comes of it we'll go straight back to England.'

Alec looked pleased when she began to speak but she saw he had no enthusiasm for a return to England. There were few places with a climate less agreeable for idling and Olga's resolution was strengthened by the awareness that it was probably the only way of keeping him with her.

'I'll go now. The less we are seen together the better. Until tomorrow.'

Alec rose to his feet to say goodbye. It was these old-fashioned gestures, drilled into him by his father, that formed part of his attraction for Olga. The company of her contemporaries, whose feelings might be genuine but whose manners were revolting, had given her a disproportionate liking for superficial courtesies. The dark, brooding child at the orphanage had watched with envy the easy grace of visiting patrons and even then resented the barriers that would prevent her from ever attaining the cultivation and self-confidence to share their facile assumption of superiority. She could never expect to be chosen to present the bouquet to visiting royalty or indeed to emerge from the rank and file in any way. Alec's school had at least helped him to an easy manner. He had no wish to become a business success but in bars he had no difficulty in joining such men as an equal socially and securing free drinks.

When she had gone Alec sank back on the bench with an unusual feeling of foreboding. He was not given to thought for the morrow but he couldn't help doubting whether real luck was to come his way at last. As far as he could see there was no danger, no risk even in failure. It was too good to be true. He watched the cruise ship whose passengers were now disporting themselves on the toboggan ride, cramming the tourist shops on the front or consuming yet another large meal at a noted restaurant. Out of the blue came back some lines from the volume of poetry that crammed his memory:

> Thou camest with thy hollow scheme,
> But sail, O architect of dream.

If only he could afford to sail away on that ship leaving hollow schemes and Olga's intense presence behind. He was intended to be a lotus eater. Had his grandfather really frittered away an inheritance? He talked as if there had been a time when he was wealthy but even as a small child Alec had realised he did not always differentiate between fact and fancy. It was what the small boy had loved about him. Listening to him was like living in a fantasy world. His father was completely different – a hard disillusioned man who reluctantly supported *his* father. Alec had seen that he humiliated the old man unnecessarily and would put his hand sympathetically in his as they walked to the park away from the last bitter insult from his son. And in the park all would be forgotten in stories of pirates and buried treasure more convincing than those in the old copies of the *Boys' Own* that he found in the attic. These were one of the few possessions his grandfather had retained when he joined his son in the little terrace house so different from the country mansion in which Alec believed the old man had been brought up.

132

Alec was not too pleased to see Davenport walking along the front where he must pass close in front of him. He would prefer to avoid him till his and Olga's scheme was completed. He did not under-estimate Davenport's shrewdness and had a feeling that their short conversation in the taxi had revealed more than he intended. It was too late to take evasive action so he looked up and smiled as if he had just caught sight of him.

'Join me for a cup of coffee?' Davenport took the initiative and Alec who had never, since his escape from his father, refused an offer of food and drink accepted.

When they had been served, Alec having added a pastry to his coffee of a size and sweetness that would remove any need for another meal for some time, commented on the size of the cruise ship that had occupied his thoughts a few minutes earlier.

'I'm meeting an old friend who is travelling on it,' said Davenport. 'Would you like to come out with me and see over the ship?'

'Isn't he coming ashore?'

'No, he came on the cruise for a rest and change and shore visits tend to be rather exhausting.'

'I'd certainly like to see over the ship. I've crewed on small boats sometimes but I've never been on one of these luxury cruisers.'

As they went over to the ship they looked back at the opposite view of the city and mountains. Alec shivered.

'It's a bit chilly on the water,' Davenport said sympathetically.

'No, I'm not cold. I think something walked over my grave.' Alec gave a forced laugh as he repeated the old superstition. 'I think I shall be glad to leave Madeira. I can understand the horror of imprisonment on an island. Napoleon must have felt it on St Helena.'

Davenport looked at him curiously.

'I suppose Napoleon does come to mind in this harbour. It was the beginning of the end for him.'

'Here we are.' Alec seemed glad to change the subject.

Davenport's friend was awaiting them on deck. He was a frail-looking old man, a don of an older generation than Davenport. He introduced him to Alec, who, American fashion repeated Professor Bosworth's name and gave his own.

'My young friend would like to see over the ship,' Davenport said and Bosworth called a steward and asked him to arrange it.

As he departed Bosworth said, 'Good-looking young fellow. Who is he?'

'I don't really know but he might share your interest in Napoleon.'

'Really? He must join us for lunch.'

Bosworth called for drinks and the two settled down to the university gossip, which Bosworth relied on Davenport to keep him up to date with. An hour passed quickly and Alec returned to thank Bosworth charmingly for his tour.

'Stay to lunch. Stay to lunch.' Bosworth had reached the age that tends to repetition.

Alec hesitated.

'Come alone. Come along. I shan't take a refusal.'

Alec fell in behind them and they went to the dining-room.

Few people had remained on the boat but several tables were occupied. At one were two extremely well dressed people, a man and a woman. Davenport realised it was the clothes that struck him first though when he looked again he noticed that they were both handsome in a characterless sort of way.

'I see you are looking at the Middletons,' Bosworth had used the privileges of old age to get to know all about everyone on board. He was not afraid to use the direct question to find out what he wanted to know and sometimes repeated aloud information that had been confided to him in a whisper.

'Yes. They look familiar but I can't remember ever seeing them before.' Davenport was relieved to see their table was far enough away for Bosworth not to be overheard unless he shouted. As he had never had to do this to make his presence felt, his friends were saved from one of the embarrassments of conversing with the aged in public.

'They are an eccentric pair. They are brother and sister and are famous designers of clothes, I suppose, judging by the way they dress. Yes, brother and sister, brother and sister, but they never speak to one another.'

'Have they quarrelled?'

'Don't know but I've never seen them speak.'

'I think I've heard of them,' said Alec. 'They work together but never discuss their work. They exchange briefcases and I suppose modify each other's designs. They are enormously rich so I suppose the exchange is a successful publicity stunt. They advertise by avoiding advertisement. I suppose it gives their clients an illusion of exclusiveness.'

'Extraordinary. Extraordinary. And what brought you to Madeira? Like the place? Like the place?'

'It's quite pleasant, said Alec noncommittally.

'Ah, you youngsters see too much too soon. I can remember being thrilled going down the toboggan slope with a pretty girl when I was young.'

Perhaps the contrast between Bosworth's light-hearted youth with a naïve if newly emancipated flapper of the twenties and Olga and him struck Alec dumb. He made no reply.

Meanwhile Davenport was smiling to himself. The Middletons must be the suspicious couple of Rhoda's plane journey. He looked forward to enlightening her and laughing over the criminal suspicions they had entertained.

'I believe you are interested in Napoleon's visit to Madeira, Bosworth,' said Davenport seeing that Alec's interest had gone back to the excellent lunch he was enjoying in spite of the pastry consumed over coffee. How nice to be young enough to have no problems of digestion.

'Yes I am, yes I am. I believe there was more in it than met the eye. Conquerors always suppress all they can about the conquered. It was very fishy that a popular governor was sacked just for addressing Napoleon as "Your Majesty". There was no question of the governor's loyalty to the crown and they had to reinstate him by popular demand. There is no proof but I think Napoleon must have given him some confidences that he refused to betray as a gentleman of honour.'

Alec looked up eagerly.

'My grandfather used to say ...' Here he stopped suddenly as if he had realised he was about to betray something accidentally.

'Yes, your grandfather, your grandfather ...' said Bosworth in the manner of one encouraging a shy or backward student.

'My grandfather used to talk to me about Napoleon's using Madeira as a port of call,' he said lamely.

'No, no, not Napoleon. The commander of the *Northumberland*,' Bosworth corrected. 'Napoleon had all his power and possessions stripped from him by then.'

Alec was silent.

'*All* his possessions?' asked Davenport.

135

'He probably got away with a few personal things – family miniatures, that sort of thing. But anything valuable enough to be used as a bribe to escape, no. Two Waterloos would have been more than any of the great powers could risk and the restored monarchy was never popular. If the French hadn't been as sick of war as everyone else, they wouldn't have waited till 1848 for a republic. But you don't want a history tutorial. When did your grandfather visit Madeira?' Bosworth turned to Alec again.

'Oh, ages ago. He died when I was nine so I didn't know much about his life.'

'Sad. Very sad. Children can learn a lot of history from their grandparents. My grandfather could remember the celebrations after Waterloo. He was a small child then and it was his earliest memory. He lived to be nearly a hundred but his head was clear till the day he died. He fought in the Crimean War himself. Yes, yes, it was he who started me on history. We are a long-lived family. I'm ninety, you know, ninety.'

Alec looked more appalled than admiring but Davenport said, 'You'll see your century too.'

'Perhaps, perhaps. Now let's go on deck for coffee and a brandy. Or do you young fellers like liqueurs?'

'Oh, a brandy, sir.'

'Quite right, quite right. That's what Napoleon would have had.'

Alec looked somewhat bewildered at being classified with Napoleon, but he managed to utter, 'Thank you, sir.'

They returned to their seats on deck where the old man suddenly fell asleep. Waking ten minutes later with equal suddenness he said,

'Have you seen the bust of Napoleon in the English church here?'

Alec did not reply though the question seemed to have been addressed to him. It was Davenport who related how the church had been broken into and the bust destroyed.

'Strange, very strange. Reminds me of that spiritualist feller, Conan Doyle, who wrote detective stories – only, his story had six busts of Napoleon and some murders. Glad this was a more peaceful affair. More natural in Madeira. Not a place of violence.' Thereupon he fell asleep again.

'I expect you'd like to get back on land. Bosworth will go on like this all afternoon. I want to stay as long as I can as one never knows when a visit may be one's last at his age.'

136

'I suppose not though he seems to have all his marbles.'

Alec had inadvertently slipped from his public-school to his natural manner. Davenport had noticed he seemed abstracted for some time and wanted time to think of the probable reason and what he should do himself. Alec reverted to correctness and thanked Davenport for his hospitality. Bosworth woke again to receive a grateful farewell and called a steward to arrange transport. Judging by the promptness with which the boat appeared, he had provided a handsome tip and left Alec with no necessary expenses for the day, his lunch having given him more than sufficient calories and the brandy on top of the wine leaving him sleepy and confused. No wonder the old boy kept falling asleep. Davenport would probably join him now they were alone together. Alec decided he couldn't do better than bunk down himself. He needed a clear head for the morrow though his conversation with Bosworth convinced him they were playing a very long shot. He would like to give up but now Olga had become keen he would have to go through with it.

But Davenport did not go to sleep. In the intervals of responding courteously in Bosworth's waking moments he was deep in thought. Now the Middletons were explained he believed he had a clue to what was going on and wished to save Olga and Alec from being involved. Olga had the stuff in her to make something of life even with a late start. Besides Rhoda liked her and Davenport would go a long way to prevent her being pained. Alec was harmless. The fact that he had not succumbed to drink and drugs in his way of life showed he was not viciously inclined. He took his colour from the company he kept and, as long as he was kept out of crime or violence, he might prove an adequate partner for Olga. He would meet them both the next day and see if he could get them both off to England quickly.

Having settled his mind on them he devoted the rest of the day to his old friend. They were both subject to nostalgia and thoroughly enjoyed the sporadic reminiscences of their common life. As with many old people, Bosworth's early memories were now the clearest and the recollection of the period before the First World War mixed with the later university life. It was a conversation that from time to time made Davenport think of the letters and diary of Rhoda's father but he dismissed these thoughts for, having once made up his mind on a course of action, he did not worry further about it.

It was a faculty that had greatly helped him in his working life as had a refusal to bring himself in guilty if such action proved a failure. A man (or woman) can only do his best. The past was something to enjoy not brood over. There was even relief in knowing it was unalterable.

He got back to Reid's late and decided not to get in touch with Rhoda until he had seen Olga and Alec, preferably together, next day. He fell asleep immediately and phoned Olga's hotel after breakfast. He was informed she had already gone out and he was mildly disturbed. He would have liked to get in a word of warning on the phone. He had to satisfy himself with leaving a message asking her to ring him up at Reid's as soon as possible. This meant he had to stay in the hotel so he settled down to read in his room.

Rhoda was surprised not to hear from him. She knew he had intended to give the previous day to his old friend but she had expected a phone call to arrange a meeting and tell her about his companion. In the course of the past year, Rhoda had met several of Matthew's friends and heard about more. If she had not had another engagement she would have gone with him to the ship, for she had met Bosworth and enjoyed the old man's reminiscences. He was not far from being a contemporary of her father and he recalled the world Rhoda had had no share in but that she glimpsed in her father's writings.

She had spent the previous day fulfilling an engagement with the Grantleys to attend a *festa*. Rhoda was not keen on popular festivals preferring to visit places when they were least crowded but she had been often told that they were dying out so regarded the expedition in the light of supporting a dying species. Moreover, as the festival in question was to take place in Canical she was taking the opportunity of renewing her acquaintance with the Heathcotes whom they could pick up en route. Though she would be a fifth wheel, she did not expect to feel it with two such civilised couples as the Grantleys and the Heathcotes but she would certainly have enjoyed it more had Matthew been able to come.

Rhoda was aware of an atmosphere of suppressed excitement when she got into the Grantleys' taxi and noticed immediately that Frank had lost the aura of failure that had hung about him on previous meetings.

'He's got a job,' said Harriet triumphantly.

'Congratulations. Is it one you were hoping for?'

Frank smiled. 'Better than I could have hoped for. It is not with any of the new enterprises that are springing up like mushrooms and may disappear with equal rapidity. I am to be a tax consultant with one of the oldest established firms on the island. It is a new appointment as a result of Portugal's entry into the Common Market so I'm not doing anyone else out of a job.'

Harriet broke in, 'They are lucky to get him as his experience is exactly what they want and he had been out so short a time that he can almost pick up where he left off.'

'Well, a festival is the right sort of celebration for the occasion. I suppose you will now start house hunting. Will you live in Funchal?'

'It may be too expensive. We quite like this time-share apartment we're renting. Frank isn't a great gardener and if I get a job too I shall have enough of other people's gardens so we may just take an apartment in the same complex. It will be handy for the family when we are on holiday in England.'

Harriet was bubbling. The covert air of anxiety with which she had regarded her husband had gone. It was almost like seeing two people suddenly recovered from crippling illness. After all, thought Rhoda, stress *is* a crippling illness and her spirits lifted to match theirs.

They had covered the journey between Funchal and the airport too often to find special interest in the scenery. It was just as well as they could hardly spare attention to look at it. However, once they had picked up the Heathcotes the short journey beyond Machico was new to them. Though long enough retired to have put behind them the stresses of the world of work, the Heathcotes had sufficient imagination to share the pleasure of the others in the new prospect and over lunch they toasted the younger couple.

The *festa* proved more enjoyable than Rhoda had expected. Congenial company made a considerable difference to her usual attitude and, as they were able to sit in a wayside cafe to watch the procession – it was much less tiring than such occasions normally prove. It was, moreover, a genuine traditional festival not an affair revived for the tourist trade. Local people were enjoying a family holiday and the children must have long looked forward to the dressing up and dancing that had been part of their parents' lives before them. Fatigue and fretfulness were not yet visible and Rhoda and her companions enjoyed the gaiety without sophistication

139

which had disappeared even in their own villages while they were still children. The dark eyes and the brightly coloured costumes reflected a society where children were still children. Their parents could not afford computer games or specialised equipment and they did not know the Joneses with whom their less fortunate contemporaries had to keep up.

They stopped at the hotel in Machico to have tea with the Heathcotes and talked over the afternoon's experience. Rhoda concluded with a tribute to the wisdom of Solomon who asked neither for long life nor riches nor vengeance. How many of the world's problems would be solved if all had the motivation of his prayer and leaders were able to distinguish between good and bad.

'Didn't shine in private life though,' said Douglas Heathcote mischievously.

'I suppose none of us would be pleased if we got all we prayed for.' Agnes made her contribution. 'If the Kingdom of Heaven came today the majority would be stateless.'

'Not even a British passport would be effective.'

'It would however *look* better than the others.'

'Yes, we are still superior to the rest of the world in that respect. I'm always cheered when I look at the sturdy cover and gold lettering. It would take quite a strong frontier guard to tear it up.'

They regarded one another with the complacency of a nation with a great past without the realisation that they had lost it. Though aware their country was no longer one of the great powers, the intelligence had never got through to their emotions. 'Land of hope and glory' came more naturally than 'Jerusalem' as Blake would have been the first to recognise if the former had been composed in his time.

The party broke up in amity and a medley of thanks one to the other for a pleasant day. Rhoda and the Grantleys sank back in their taxi with sighs of satisfaction. None of them could foresee what would be the consequences of the all-day engagements of Rhoda and Davenport nor perhaps would it have changed the destiny of those who passed through the postern of fate on the morrow.

Chapter 15

The Splendour of Things Lost

Rhoda decided that for once she would take the initiative and rang up Matthew ostensibly to ask how he had enjoyed meeting his old friend. He explained why he was still in his room and had not got in touch with her.

'Would you like to come up here for coffee? It will be lovely out on the terrace now the rain has cleared and I can let them know at the desk where I am if Miss Bayne does ring.'

'I should like that,' said Rhoda. 'I'll be with you in about a quarter of an hour. It won't take longer than a quarter of an hour to walk up.'

Matthew met her at the main door. Rhoda blessed his sensitive perception in realising she would not want to enter alone after the fiasco of her first tea at Reid's. In fact she wondered if she would ever feel able to enter the hotel alone again. Perhaps the sensation, so unusual for her of being *persona non grata* would wear off in time or be totally exorcised by Matthew's companionship.

'I've arranged about the phone call so we'll go straight to the terrace.'

He had evidently arranged about the coffee too as it appeared immediately they sat down. Davenport had made himself *persona very much grata* with the waiters at Reid's and Rhoda guessed it was more by his genuine courtesy than by the size of tips to which they must have been accustomed.

'This is delightful.' As she spoke Rhoda looked over the wide expanse of blue sea and then smiled affectionately at Matthew.

What luck it had been that they had happened to be at the same guest house in Switzerland. His friendship had enriched her life. Oddly enough Matthew was thinking the same thing. He had always had plenty of friends but the women had usually been wives of friends and it was to his credit that the wives became friends. There were so many women who were jealous of their husband's wider friendships that they cut them off from them. Rhoda was the first single woman who had become a welcome companion. She was intelligent enough to share his interests and the fact that she was a pleasure to look at was a bonus. Rhoda might have said the same thing of Matthew. Unlike most men of his age he had not gone to seed and was fortunate enough to be neither bald nor fat. In mutual understanding they sat and drank their coffee.

'How was Professor Bosworth?'

'Quite up to standard. The voyage has already done him good. He enjoys getting out among people outside the academic world. He's a real observer and of course on board ship he can find out all there is to be known about his fellow passengers. He has solved a mystery for you.'

'For *me*?'

'Well, I was glad to have it solved too. It's the mystery of the exchanged briefcases.'

'No, really? Is Mark Pemberley over here?' She referred to the Customs and Excise officer who had involved her in her Swiss adventure.

'No there is no question of drugs or smuggling. They are designers who use an advertising ploy of not being on speaking terms with one another so instead of consulting about their designs they exchange them for alteration and correction in their briefcases.'

'How absurd.'

'Perhaps it isn't. One is less likely to be exasperated by alterations on paper than if one is pontificating to the other about the superiority of his ideas. Anyway they are among the most affluent of the nouveau riche. Presumably an air of mystery pays off better than the uncompleted comparatives of advertisements. Instead of being "better" they are "unique".'

'But if everyone knows . . .'

'Bosworth isn't everyone. Besides I expect the appearance on board ship was an intentional leak and they will next have a reconciliation and appear on a TV programme to show they are now speaking to one another.'

'I suppose nothing is too idiotic in self-advertisement. The only aim is to be different. It's the same objective that has lowered the standards of art and drama – especially drama. If it weren't for the present daft practice of passing laws about everything I might lobby for a law that Shakespeare must be played straight for the next decade.'

'It might be better to pray for some new playwrights and then the classics would be less at the mercy of novelty crazy directors. But to get back to the Middletons . . .'

'The Middletons?'

'Oh, didn't I mention the name? They are your now no longer a mysterious couple; brother and sister by the way.'

'That accounts for their resemblance to one another. I thought perhaps it was just the image of affluent nullity.'

'You are very severe on the affluent.'

'Especially as I am comfortably off myself, you might add. I am not against prosperity in itself but against the power for evil that it gives to individuals and when not power the insidious influence of self-centred greed.'

'You don't agree with the Victorian idea that the rich should shed their superfluity on the poor for whom there is the biblical authority that they would be always with us?'

Davenport was speaking tongue in cheek and Rhoda knew it but pursued the point in all seriousness.

'That is what cut them off from the church. The distortion of Christian teaching in favour of the rich must have been one of the chief causes of the desertion of the poor when they emigrated to the cities. No longer compelled to go to church by their landlords, they looked on rejecting it as an escape from slavery, hence the atheism of some powerful working-class movements. It was not so bad in Britain as elsewhere because in the country there was usually a personal relationship between landlord and tenant. The poor were persons not just hands but urban poor had to wait till now to find Christianity was for them. Of course the situation is clarified when governments murder archbishops.'

'Yes, extremes are enlightening but seldom achieve anything constructive.'

They sat in silence for a few minutes.

143

'To return to personal relationships, I fear Miss Bayne cannot intend to get in touch with me. Shall I ring her hotel and check whether she has had my message and if she doesn't intend to follow it up we might as well go out to lunch?'

'I'm sorry to have landed you with this bother.'

'Don't feel that. I have become interested in her and her young man. I've more to tell you about him, by the way. Are you happy to stay here or will you come up to my room?'

'Oh, here, thank you. It will probably be the last time this holiday that I shall be enjoying this view.'

Rhoda enjoyed the view but with an underlying feeling of disquiet. She had been so sure that Olga wanted a new beginning in her life but the failure to use the help at hand suggested opposite influences at work. When Matthew came back it was to say Olga had not returned to her hotel since she had gone out that morning so she had not received his message. The probability was that she would not ring up till evening, so they set off to town.

Rhoda did not bring up the subject of Alec as there was no need to try to talk against the noise of traffic when they would have the whole of lunch time to chat in comfort. Instead they turned from the sad music of humanity to the roses and butterflies that made the stroll into town cheerfully colourful.

'We'll try somewhere new.' Matthew turned into a cool dark room frequented by businessmen rather than by tourists. Since they came to talk over business, it would be a better spot for conversation than a tourist resort where the customers tended to talk more loudly and continuously than in this quiet café. They ordered a light lunch and Rhoda indulged in her usual sweet Madeira.

'Have you seen much of Pixie and Constance recently?'

Rhoda's Madeira had recalled to Matthew Constance's very dry sherry.

'Yes, we still dine together. We shall all be leaving the island at about the same time. It's odd to think I didn't know either of them three weeks ago.'

'And three years ago I didn't know you.'

'Yes, I was thinking just how lucky I was to have met you when I did. If it had been when mother was alive I should never have got to know you.'

Matthew looked startled.

'Was she so very possessive?'

144

'No, not exactly. It was just that any man who came into her radius became *her* friend. It was not intentional – it just happened. I sometimes wonder if it was why she married father. She was such a vivid personality she needed someone muted to complement her.'

Matthew made no comment. It was his belief that Rhoda's mother must have been a human python. How else account for Rhoda remaining unmarried? Davenport was a perceptive person but too much a man of his time and class to imagine a woman might *prefer* a single life though it was what he had elected for himself after his brief marriage ended.

He changed the subject.

'I met Alec yesterday. I took him on board with me to see over the ship and we had lunch with Bosworth. He's an odd mixture. He must have some sort of public-school background. They talked about Napoleon's connection with the island.'

'And that's one of Professor Bosworth's interests isn't it? I can imagine Alec having some of the con man's readiness to be all things to all men.'

Matthew hesitated. It was clear that Rhoda had a prejudice against Alec or he might have pointed out that on that evidence St Paul was an earlier con man. He decided that he would wait before he said more until he had a chance to talk to Alec again. If he could arrange to meet him and Olga together he might get his suspicions confirmed or allayed. Meanwhile there was little to be gained by speculating further with Rhoda.

'What makes you think he's a public-school man?' Never having been to school, Rhoda had a sort of 'Playing fields of Eton' conception of public schools.

'He can speak very well and he has that sort of ease of manner that boarding-school life produces. One *has* to learn how to get on with all sorts of people.'

'I see.' Rhoda was not really interested in Alec except in so far as he influenced Olga.

Davenport suggested that as they were near Olga's hotel they might call in and see if she had returned and Rhoda agreed the more willingly as she felt she had been somewhat ungracious about Alec. As conversation is impossible in city centres that admit traffic, they walked in silence. Davenport felt a peculiar urgency to get to Olga as if by so doing he could prevent some disaster. Perhaps he should have made more effort in the morning after his first real meeting with Alec. He was, however, fated to delay. As they were passing the cathedral they met Constance and Pixie who were bubbling over with news that they must impart to someone.

'Will you have a coffee with us?' Constance asked with extraordinary eagerness.

'Of course.' It did not occur to Rhoda to consult Matthew first. She was not aware of his premonitions and assumed they were going to spend the afternoon together with no limits as to time. Davenport was tied by conventional good manners to follow the three ladies and did so with a mental shrug. No one is indispensable and he had no assurance that even if he saw Olga she would alter her plans in any way for his arguments.

He joined the waiter in pulling out chairs for the ladies and ordered coffee. As they evidently had good news to impart, he suggested a liqueur as well to Pixie's delight. She was not used to being the centre of attention and Constance's pride in her success was rare enough to arouse an almost schoolgirlish excitement. In fact the emotion she felt was very similar to that she had felt when made captain of the first tennis team at school when Constance had shown a like approbation.

Constance spoke. 'Pixie is to be in the next Honours list.'

Rhoda's and Matthew's congratulations came in unison.

'For services to the community, I'm sure,' said Rhoda.

'Yes,' Pixie blushed with pleasure.

'And she's earned it,' said Constance loyally. 'Both in the village and the county. And there have been national and international events that wouldn't have gone so well but for her.'

'That's splendid. When did you hear?'

'Well of course you get a strong hint beforehand so we had a friend looking out for the letter and she rang me up this morning and read it to me. I can't believe it's really true but it will be a great thrill going to the palace.'

'We've been to royal garden parties but naturally there are so many people there you barely get a glimpse of the queen. Pixie will meet her as an individual now.'

Rhoda warmed to Constance. Though she obviously liked the reflected glory, she wanted even more for others to appreciate Pixie's abilities. Pixie herself was in a dream. Awards had never entered her mind as a possible consequence of her activities, so it was all a delightful surprise in which Constance's unalloyed

146

admiration played as great a part as the honour itself. Rhoda found herself hoping that it would never be stolen to sell to a collector. She knew of more than one case where this had happened and wondered at the mentality of people who could buy them.

'This calls for more than coffee. Shall we dine together tonight with the appropriate champagne?' Davenport offered the invitation in good faith but he was also looking for a reason to leave the two ladies now and get on to Olga's hotel. It suddenly seemed a matter of life and death to get in touch with her.

Pixie accepted the invitation with almost giggling glee, Constance with more sober correctness.

'Tonight at eight then?' Davenport rose to his feet. 'At Reid's.' He managed to wait without visible impatience through the thanks and *au revoirs* and, as soon as the others had turned in the opposite direction, he took Rhoda's arm and set off at a brisk pace to her astonishment.

'I have a presentiment we are too late,' he said, catching sight of her expression.

'Too late for what?' She was bewildered. Her mind was still on Pixie.

'I don't know, but since talking to Alec yesterday I have a feeling he and Olga were planning something and I had hoped to warn them off.'

'But why today?'

'I think they are deciding one way or another.'

Before Rhoda could question further and, in the difficult background of crowds and traffic she had barely followed what he had said so far, they were at the door of Olga's hotel.

'No. I don't think Miss Bayne has been back since breakfast. Her key is still in the pigeon hole and I have been on duty and have not seen her pass.'

'You would recognise her?' Davenport asked the receptionist.

'Oh yes, she has been here longer than most of the other guests. She was here for a week before her friend arrived. I don't know where he is staying but he has called for her several times and I have seen them in town together. Do you still wish her to have this message when she comes in?' pointing to the scrap of paper with the key.

'Yes,' he hesitated, then said 'Yes' again.

Rhoda looked at him anxiously.

147

'What *is* the matter?'

Davenport was silent for a moment.

'Would you mind if we went up to the church before going back?'

'No, of course not. Wait till we get there and you can tell me all about it in peace and quiet.'

Davenport was grateful for her understanding reception of his unusual irresolution. Rhoda was really concerned. In all the time she had known him this was the first when he had betrayed anxiety. Usually his great charm was the outward reflection of a quiet mind. He had taken Olga's problems in his stride. Why should he be apprehensive now? Rhoda mentally blamed Alec for his mood which did not lessen her prejudice against him.

Had they known, the postern of fate had already been passed. It was Alec who had become dubious in the end. He had liked Bosworth and there came a change in perspective with meeting someone who was ninety and still enjoying life, who had interests through which he would maintain vitality until death. Alec looked back on his twenty-six years without any objective. His most enjoyable times had been up to the age of nine when his feckless grandfather had provided affection and at least verbal adventure. The death of his father had passed unnoticed. Alec had been in India when it happened and had heard about it almost by accident three months later. Characteristically his father's careful savings had disappeared in the Stock Exchange's periodic meteoric declines when the greed of the small saver led to total loss while the wealthy hedged their bets. He lived in Alec's memory only in contrast to his grandfather, a memory without affection and without interest.

He met Olga ready to back down, take the plane to England and begin a different sort of life. He remembered his fluent pen in schooldays. With all the rubbish printed nowadays he could surely gain a livelihood by writing. He contemplated a permanent relationship with Olga whose more saleable skills could keep them going until he established himself. His fantasies were no more realistic than his grandfather's adventures but they converted him temporarily from his criminal intent to steal. He had no chance, however, of imposing them on Olga's stronger character and longer experience in the world of work.

'Who do you know in the publishing world?' Her words destroyed the central fabric of his dream. He had no useful connections. He had no confidence in his abilities. His only asset was his

148

superficial charm and that would not outlive his youth. Against Olga's determination he stood no chance. She had deliberately kept out of touch with Davenport. St Augustine's universally captivating prayer, 'Lord, make me good but not yet,' had won the day. They could become good afterwards. Meanwhile why miss this one chance? It could well come to nothing like his previous attempt and they would be none the worse. No one would be harmed and if they did nothing the lost opportunity would haunt them all their lives. There was enough truth in this to persuade Alec from his new and shallow resolution. Looked at in the light of one of his grandfather's adventures, it would be quite entertaining. They made their plan. They would go to church at lunchtime when nobody was likely to be about. Though not so resolute as the French in clinging to a civilised lunchtime, the Portuguese retained it to some extent. If anyone was there, Olga would distract attention while he went ahead. It couldn't fail; it might succeed.

They arrived at the church at about the time that Rhoda and Davenport were beginning lunch only a few hundred yards away. There seemed to be no one about but they knew it was likely that someone might be around, able to observe them even if out of their sight. Olga paused outside the entrance as if to find the best place from which to take a photograph. Alec wandered casually in paus- ing by a display of paperbacks in the porch and entering the side door. He was holding a large plastic bag of the type in which travellers' carry their haphazard possessions. Olga moved on to the porch from which she could watch the garden and see the interior of the church. There was no one inside. Alec moved swiftly, found the door of the vestry unlocked and, miraculously, there was what he sought on the table in full view. In a moment it was in his bag and he was out in the main body of the church moving fast.

Another five minutes and all would be well. Then he heard children's voices. If they were alone he thought there would be no trouble. Neither he nor Olga knew enough of children to under- stand their curiosity and persistence in satisfying it. And these were the rector's children. Olga could not get rid of them and Alec waited in the nave undecided whether to keep out of sight or walk out nonchalantly as if he had no connection with Olga. He was defeated by a four year old. Olga had no attraction for Bea, who in pure mischief, dodged into the church knowing this was forbidden without the company of one of her parents. The boys knew their duty and followed to drag her out. But Bea was in a perverse mood. She bolted up the aisle getting behind Alec who stood paralysed. Olga halted at the door equally unsure of the next move. Bea, peaking round Alec, caught sight of the familiar contents of Alec's bag.

'Ooh. Look.'

Mark and John rushed up.

'That's my dad's. You mustn't touch it,' said Mark.

Alec improvised hastily.

'I'm taking it to your house.'

'We'll go with you,' and the three children lined up by him.

He looked with horror. He knew nothing about children except that they could make a hell of a row and *that* he didn't want. Turning helplessly to Olga he mutely asked for a solution to the problem. It was not an occasion for pulling a knife which would have been the quick method of some of his contemporaries for getting rid of unwanted company. Olga rose to the occasion.

'You go on,' she said. 'The kids can show me round this lovely church.' She beamed with synthetic interest. They stared at her unmoved.

'You can't take Dad's holy box out of the church,' Mark said firmly.

It was the box that had once contained the statue of Napoleon and which was now used for a portable communion set. The basketwork container projecting from the plastic bag made it easily recognisable and the children had seen it so often in their father's hand as he set off to hospital that they could not be deceived. Balked with it actually in his hand, needing only half an hour to get it to Olga's room, search and return it, Alec raised his hand to strike. With an unexpected twist, John snatched the container from Alec's hand and darted up towards the gallery. Alec turned to follow and fell flat on his face over Mark's foot which had suddenly intruded into his path. Losing her head at the thought of losing the loot, Olga pursued John upstairs followed by Bea who arrived after a slower negotiation of the stairs to see Olga with the box in her grip as she twisted John's arm. 'Ouch,' he exclaimed involuntarily, though training in the inner-city streets had given him the ability to conceal pain. Still it was a nasty twist. Bea indignantly drew back her foot and administered a hefty kick to Olga's shin with her stout little sandal. It was Olga's turn to say 'Ouch', but Bea was now well out

150

of reach having learned from her brothers that reciprocal treatment followed if she went too far.

As Olga clutched her ankle, Mark seized the handle of the box and dashed round a pillar. She pursued him limping somewhat and handicapped by Bea who knew how to run interference for the boys. Meanwhile, below in the nave, Alec had got to his feet and aimed a hefty clout at Mark who sidestepped to avoid a blow that would have felled him. Realising this and now feeling rather frightened, Mark fled upstairs pursued somewhat clumsily by Alec still shaken by his fall and from rage at being outmanoeuvred by two seven year olds.

John was still dodging Olga round the pillars while she was handicapped by Bea's firm grip on her skirt which could be removed only be damaging the child to an extent she was unwilling to risk. She wanted the box but not enough to face a charge of assault.

'The man's coming,' shouted Mark breathlessly and, as he appeared, the children realised the odds were overwhelming unless they could keep out of reach.

'Fetch Daddy,' called Mark to Bea. Releasing her hold on Olga's skirt, Bea ran for the stairs, butting Alec in the stomach en route. Still bewildered by the sudden disintegration of their plans, Alec let the child go by and instead of going after her, when she could easily have been overtaken on the stairs, he made for John and the box hoping for a snatch and a quick getaway.

John, with promise of future prowess on the rugby field, passed the box to Mark who made off to the other side of the gallery at the double, John meanwhile dodging about between his two opponents. This hide and seek continued for a few minutes, but, in spite of the boys' advantage in knowing the terrain and in being small enough to take advantage of the confined spaces, they were bound to be overtaken. The box was in John's hand when Alec grasped his shoulder. Mark was not near enough for a pass and, in desperation, John hurled the box over the gallery rail to the floor of the nave. It landed at the feet of the astounded chaplain and broke into pieces. White with horror at the sacrilege, Mark and John peered over, looking at their father not at the broken box, from the base of which had spilled a glittering necklace.

For a moment everyone froze in two separate tableaux, one in the gallery and one in the nave where Bea and Olivia had arrived as the box fell. Alex was the first to move. The sight of the necklace upset the balance of his mind. He rushed down the stairs and regardless of the possibilities of explaining away the situation, he turned towards the shattered box with hand outstretched. The chaplain, seeing the look of tragic desperation on his face, raised his hand almost automatically in a blessing. Alec paused, glimpsed the expression of pity on his face and turned. He rushed out of the church and into the street. Roscommon and Olivia ran towards the street, Olivia first calling to the boys to stay with Bea. Olga could not move. The boys glanced at her doubtfully and ran down the stairs to grab Bea. They need not have worried. Her eye had been caught by the diamond necklace which would enhance so well her costume as Princess of Wales. Before the boys could reach her she had picked it up and draped it complacently round her neck.

The last of the necklaces that the Emperor had acquired for his sisters and which he had hoped would be used as a bribe for his escape was being treated as a child's toy. Her parents reached the street to find a crowd already gathered about Alec's broken body. There was nothing they could do for him. He had passed through the Postern of Fate to Death's Cavern. The chaplain knelt beside him and prayed. The unhappy driver of the lorry that had killed him protested over and over again that it was not his fault. Those in the crowd who had seen the accident supported him.

'He rushed out straight under the bonnet.'

'He came out of the gate without looking.'

'He hurled himself in the middle of the road.'

It was clear that there would be plenty of his compatriots to exonerate the driver from blame but it was too soon for him to realise their vindication. In a state of shock he continued to assert his innocence and those around him to assure him he was blameless. It was not until a policeman arrived and began the routine for dealing with street accidents that the reiteration stopped. The crowd was cleared. The chaplain, in view of his office and the fact that the victim was British, was allowed to stay. Olivia had already gone back to the children.

The ambulance arrived and the body was placed on a stretcher. It was at that moment that Davenport and Rhoda turned into the street.

'Oh dear, there's been an accident,' said Rhoda seeing police and ambulance together. Davenport stood still for a moment. His premonition had been fulfilled. He was too late. They moved on, seeing Roscommon.

Davenport held out his hand to stop the stretcher.

'Let me see,' he said.

The stretcher bearers paused and one of the policemen nodded permission. Davenport turned back the blanket. The face was little injured.

'You know him?'

'Yes.'

Davenport turned to Rhoda.

'Please go to the church. I think you will find Olga there.'

In shocked silence Rhoda walked through the gates.

Davenport told the police the name of the dead man and asked if he could accompany the body in the ambulance with the chaplain. The police agreed asking both to come afterwards to the police station where a senior officer would interview them. Their job was to deal with the street scene. Since a tourist was involved the rest would be in the hands of the higher powers.

Meanwhile Rhoda had joined Olivia in the church, where the children were endeavouring to explain how they had come by the box and how it had come to be broken. Used as she was to sorting out their narratives, Olivia was still so bewildered that she had not even thought of removing the necklace from Bea's neck. The boys were in a state of shock and the disappearance of their father when they needed to tell him all about it confused them. This, however, was a situation Olivia had had to cope with often as Barnabas's parish demanded more attention than he could give his family. She took them to sit on the steps outside and, disregarding Bea who was parading up and down waving a patronising hand to the imaginary crowds who stood admiring her new necklace, she began to sort out what had happened.

Soon afterwards Rhoda arrived.

'Is Olga here?'

Olivia looked bewildered.

'There's a lady up in the gallery.' Mark was obviously pleased that someone else could cope with her and they could keep their mother. Rhoda ran up to the gallery. Olga was lying on the floor unconscious. She had heard the terrible cry and the screaming of brakes and guessed that she was left alone. Rhoda called to Olivia

153

for water and, leaving the children with the assurance that Daddy would not be cross and she would explain everything to him, she brought up the water and together they brought Olga back to a dazed consciousness. But what to do with her? She insisted she was all right and wanted to go back to her hotel. It was such a short distance away that Rhoda decided it would be the best thing to do, leaving Olivia to her own family. Olga had to be told that Alec was dead though Rhoda was pretty sure that she already knew it. Olivia was able to supply brandy and with its aid, Olga walked quite firmly down the stairs and out of the church. She ignored the boys who drew away from her while Bea stopped her processing to gaze. Rhoda wondered how on earth Bea came to be wearing what looked like a genuine diamond necklace. Rhoda's mother had possessed one and this looked like the real thing. However, there were too many Alice-in-Wonderland events to cope with at once so, saying goodbye to Olivia, she promised to ring her up later. Taking Olga's arm firmly she led her away. Olga had not spoken a word since she had demanded to go back to the hotel.

Olivia locked the church and went back to the rectory with the children. She started the boys off on a game of chess and tactfully removed the necklace from Bea explaining that as it came from Daddy's box, she would have to ask him if she could wear it. Bea decided this was reasonable and accepted some bright red beads from her mother as prettier than the diamonds and returned to her imaginary royal world.

Rhoda got Olga to bed and insisted on calling the doctor who had attended her, chiefly because his English was excellent. He diagnosed shock caused by having been told of the accident nearby, administered a sedative and said the patient would be all right by morning. Rhoda paid the fee on the spot assuming it would not occur to Olga. Once Olga was asleep, there was nothing more she could do, so she arranged with reception that someone should take up Olga's breakfast at a fairly early hour and see if she was quite well. As she left a handsome tip she had no doubt that this would be done and asking the receptionist to get her a taxi she went back to her hotel feeling exhausted.

She knew Davenport would ring up remembering with horror the celebration dinner that had been arranged with Pixie and Constance. At about seven, Matthew rang. As might be expected of him,

154

he had already arranged with Pixie to postpone the celebration till after their return to England and have it in his Oxford home.

'I don't know whether you want to dine with them as usual but I told them about the accident so they will understand if you want to stay in your room.'

Rhoda accepted the alternative with relief and said she would ring Pixie's room and tell her.

'I'll call for you tomorrow morning,' Matthew went on and, in view of his weary tone, Rhoda asked no questions.

'I shall look forward to seeing you. Good night and I hope you will sleep.'

'Thank you. Good night.'

Chapter 16

One Brief Vision Gone

Next afternoon Rhoda and Davenport sat at a table in the spacious and empty bar of her hotel. It was the perfect Madeiran day, warm and sunny but a little breeze prevented sultriness. All the guests at the hotel were disposed around the swimming pool or away on excursions. They had the place to themselves but as yet they had said nothing beyond the conventional greeting. Rhoda thought of the waiters at the hotel in Machico who had enquired with such seeming solicitude if one had slept well. She felt she had failed to communicate the same caring to Matthew, who looked tired and sad.

'You didn't know his name?'

Rhoda was puzzled for a moment, then,

'You mean Alec? No, that was how Olga introduced him. I no longer try to resist this Christian-name-only fashion unless it involves someone I expect to get to know.'

'He was Alexander Seaton.'

'Seaton? You don't mean . . .'

'Yes. He was the grandson of the "young Seaton" of your father's diary.'

Rhoda was silent as she recalled what had been said of the Seatons. Another 'young Seaton' marred in the making? As so often happened now in their deepening friendship, Matthew read her thoughts.

'The weakness skipped a generation. His father was a hard insensitive man like the colonel but without his better qualities. Alec

156

loved his feckless grandfather who stuffed him with adventure and treasure stories but died before Alex was old enough to see them for what they were.'

'You mean that necklace that Bea was wearing really was a Napoleonic treasure?'

Davenport smiled slightly for the first time.

'So it provided a note of reality in Bea's game? Well, it's in a bank vault now, having brought Alec to his death. The Napoleonic treasure must have been one of his grandfather's favourite stories but nothing would have come of it if he hadn't followed Olga to Madeira and repeated it to her. She was embittered and eager for a new way of life and must have thought it worth investigating. Alec broke into the church as his grandfather had done. Probably the Sherlock Holmes story of *The Six Napoleons* led him to smash the statue to no purpose. The bust could be believed to have sentimental value for his sister Pauline – it had no other value – and had she followed him as far as Madeira, it would have been handed over to her by the governor as an act of courtesy. Napoleon would expect Pauline to look further than the ostensible contents. The necklace, of course, was concealed in the base.

'And it would never have been found but for the little boys smashing the box in their efforts to defend what they thought to be their father's property.'

Davenport ordered more tea as they sat pondering the succession of accidents that had led to Alec's brief vision of prosperity and destroyed his short life.

'When did you learn his name?'

'He gave it automatically to Bosworth. Alec was like a chameleon and took his colour from his surroundings. Bosworth is a scholar-gentleman of the old school and Alec had been drilled into conventional manners by his father and school. To a man of Bosworth's generation it would have been unnatural to say a forename. As soon as he said "Seaton" a number of things fell into place and Alex revealed a lot more in conversation with Bosworth. The old man has a way of getting confidences without appearing curious. He was a famous personal tutor in his day. Even now you'll find middle-aged men recalling having been in one of his vacation reading parties with as much pride as if it was an Honours List. He handpicked those he took so it was a cachet for them.'

Rhoda was glad to hear him wandering from the immediate subject to pleasanter recollections. But he soon came back to Alec.

'That's why I was so anxious to get in touch with Olga yesterday. I guessed she had abstracted and returned the diary the day when she came twice to see you. She admitted it to me when I saw her this morning. I think she was ashamed of what she had done and hoped I would save her from having to tell you.'

Rhoda's expression hardened. She might forgive the physical accident but to intrude on her mental life by abstracting her father's diary was unpardonable. Davenport recognised the reaction and was glad Olga missed it. The flash of blue eyes that could intimidate a Swiss police inspector would be too much for Olga in her present state of confusion and bereavement. It was the reason he had visited her in the morning, leaving Rhoda to go later in the day. Ostensibly he went to reassure her that she would not be involved in any criminal accusation. The chaplain and he had been able to convince the police that Alec's death was an accident and they did not want a sensation created. The driver of the lorry could be fully exonerated. The emergence of a diamond necklace was a matter for church and lawyers and as, in fact, it had come to light through a child having broken a box accidentally, the two incidents could be separated. One would undoubtedly make the headlines. The other would end in a quiet funeral in the British cemetery.

Rhoda made no comment on the misuse of the diary and asked Matthew what he thought would happen to the necklace.

'Since it has been, if inadvertently, in the possession of the English church for well over a century, I think it may well turn out to be legally theirs. The whole problem will be examined by lawyers: no documentary evidence exists to prove it was Napoleon's intention to do other than give the box and its contents to the governor of Madeira. Whether any of Napoleon's descendants could put in a counter claim, I don't know.'

Rhoda commented sadly, 'I suppose it will join other famous jewels in a history of theft, murder and vanity. But at least if it's sold for the church the purchase price will go to good use.'

Matthew thought the mention of the church a good point to suggest Rhoda's visiting Olga. It is difficult to promote the church on one hand and refuse to act on its main precepts on the other.

On Matthew's offering to accompany her, Rhoda agreed to call on Olga before dinner. When the receptionist rang through to her room, Olga said she would come down to the foyer. Rhoda was struck by this unusual show of tact, which enabled them all to sit over a drink as if the call was superficially social. Olga could be depended on not to break down in public.

Rhoda's original date of departure from Funchal coincided with Olga's so her ostensible reason for calling was to offer Olga a seat in her taxi to the airport. Davenport intended to remain in Madeira for Alec's funeral. He felt it incumbent on him to represent the caring family that Alec had never possessed. A sort of empathy with the long-dead Colonel Seaton of Captain Brown's diary moved him. The last of the Seatons had perished ignominiously and pointlessly and the tragedy had been foreshadowed long before.

Olga tried to overcome her natural gaucheness to thank him.

'I would like to stay,' Davenport said gently. 'I regret my failure to help him.'

'I failed him more,' said Olga. 'His weakness exasperated me and I lost patience. If I hadn't over-persuaded him he would have given up the treasure hunt at the last minute and would still be alive. I shall always have a sense of guilt at getting off scot free.'

'Nursing a sense of guilt is futile,' Rhoda spoke sharply. 'He has lost his life. There is no need to throw away yours.'

Olga was braced to resentment which was what Rhoda intended. 'What purpose does my life serve?'

'Every individual has a value. You won't find yours by brooding over the past. Mr Davenport has not withdrawn his offer of help and it is up to you to make a fresh start. Stop feeling sorry for yourself.'

Olga glared ferociously. She had expected a softer approach from Rhoda but was provoked to return to her normal abrasive self by this treatment.

Davenport felt it had gone far enough so got up saying, 'I'll write when I get back home Miss Bayne, and you can ring me up when you are ready with your applications for college.'

Olga thanked him and blurted out to Rhoda,' 'I'm sorry. You deserved a better return from me.'

'Make it and I'll be satisfied,' replied Rhoda crisply. 'Our taxi will arrive at 1 pm so we'll meet again.'

They left Olga revived by the interest they had taken. She had to think about packing, returning to her bedsit and job hunting. She could momentarily blot out the loss of Alec. Not having witnessed the accident, she had no horrible physical memory of his death. The weakness of his nature would help to offset the absence of his companionship. She had been the prop and withdrawing it would leave her free again. When she was alone in her room tears oozed from her eyes at intervals but they were caused by pathos now rather than a sense of bereavement.

Davenport and Rhoda took a taxi to a restaurant to dine together. Rhoda felt she could not yet talk things over with Constance and Pixie and was glad to think their next meeting, except for superficial farewells, would be in Oxford. By then emotions could be recollected in tranquillity and selected memories would replace the full impact of tragedy.

'How nice to be alone together.' Rhoda was thankful for her fifty-odd years which enabled her to say exactly what she meant. If she had met Matthew at twenty she would undoubtedly have fallen in love with him and though by now they would have achieved the companionship of a shared life, it was more satisfying to her escapist nature to have the benefit without having the hard work of building a personal relationship.

Matthew smiled.

> The wheels of time are turning, turning, turning,
> The slow stream channels deep and doth not tire.

Poetry was one of their shared interests and it was seldom that they had a meal together without an exchange of quotations absorbed over a lifetime's reading. Rhoda was able to counter from Flecker,

> Death has no repose
> Warmer and deeper than the Orient sand
> Which hides the beauty and bright faith of those
> Who make the Golden Journey to Samarkand.

Alec's was not a golden journey but he had escaped young from the harsher realities of life for which he would have become progressively more unfitted.

'Yes,' said Matthew meditatively, 'like the flower people of the sixties. Long life would have been no boon for them. Some are perpetual children and I think he was a perpetual grandchild. His

160

affinity with his grandfather was his strongest link with life and his grandfather never grew up either.'

'He would have been happiest in medieval times, wandering from country to country singing and reciting poetry. With the church always in the background there would have been a roof to shelter him at night and a faith to support him without effort on his part. The twentieth century gave him a livelihood through the same talents but no purpose for living. One can't now remain rootless throughout life without becoming one of those drunken derelicts who haunt park benches and bus shelters, a living rebuke to affluence.'

'I should hate to have seen Alec drifting towards that end,' said Matthew.

'I was harsh in my judgement of him in life.' Rhoda sounded regretful.

Rhoda shivered. She had no fear of death in itself but realised her affection for Matthew was so strong that if she lost him a great deal of the joy of life would disappear. She realised she was indulging in what she had blamed Olga for – self-pity – and the more blameworthy in that its cause lay in an imaginary future whereas Olga had the present reality. She shook herself metaphorically and turned the conversation to present amenities.

By the time they had reached coffee and liqueurs, they both felt refreshed and less tired than earlier in the day. They walked up the hill and stood together looking towards the bay where sky and sea were merging together. Matthew put his hand over hers as she clasped the fence and they shared silently an instant of unity with an eternal significance. The lyrical moment was broken by the barking of dogs whose evoking of pandemonium so often destroys the peace of Madeira. They both laughed and said good night. When Rhoda reached her room, she walked out on to the balcony to recapture the scene they had shared together. Tomorrow would be a new day when she would return to the solitude of her own home at Stoneborough. Happy as she was with Matthew's friendship and in spite of her enjoyment of Madeira, she looked forward to a period of solitude. Solitude was as essential to her well-being as water and it was when she was alone that she could enjoy most, in recollection, the experience of companionship. She looked forward to meeting new-made friends again in England but for the present it was delightful to be by herself. Olga's unwanted presence

161

on the return journey would end at Gatwick. Her own Half Acre awaited her beyond. She sighed with content as she looked toward Reid's where the purple bougainvillea shadowed to darkness.

Chapter 17

Crusading Ghosts

It was a month later that Davenport's celebration dinner for Pixie Putley took place. He and Roscommon had spent some painful time after the others were in England, the chaplain on the problems of the rediscovered necklace and Davenport on Alec's death and burial. Roscommon's tour of duty in Madeira would end before the fate of the necklace was resolved so the representation of the church passed to the churchwardens and their legal aid. This saved a setback in the chaplain's recovery and was a considerable relief to Olivia.

The children soon forgot the fateful day as no mention of it was made at home. Bea once or twice enquired after the diamond necklace in spite of the substitute red beads but her brothers suppressed her having no wish themselves to remember the awful moment when the 'holy box' broke asunder at their father's feet. Bea soon after abandoned the role of the Princess of Wales for that of the Princess Royal at leisure. In imagination, she rode incessantly to the plaudits of the crowd. Mark and John being willing to be incorporated in this more active role, it lasted a long time.

As they consumed drinks in Davenport's library, Pixie, Rhoda and Matthew the conventional champagne and Constance her very dry sherry, they felt the remoteness of holiday associations. It took a little time to break the ice even after a renewal of congratulations to Pixie.

Constance sailed in where angels fear to tread.

'What happened to that impossible young woman you befriended?'

'Really, Constance,' said Pixie though the others were quite grateful for the brusque question.

'Not at all impossible,' said Davenport. 'She has a job and is going to take a degree course at the local polytechnic near her bedsit.'

'Oh, I am glad,' said Pixie warmly. 'I was sure Rhoda would bring out the best in her and it's so kind of you to help.'

Rhoda's attitude to Olga was still ambivalent. She had been able to forgive the slight push on the *levada* walk in spite of the embarrassment that followed. Olga's shamefaced confession of an act of childish spite had won pity. Rhoda had begun to realise the effect her effortless self-sufficiency could have on those who had not grown up with any confidence in their place in society. What she could not forgive was Olga's intrusion into her private life in reading her father's diary and using information in it to pursue a crime. Still she admired the courage with which Olga had made a fresh start. Davenport's support for Olga ensured that Rhoda was likely to meet her and his goodwill meant more to her than that of any other friend. They were likely to see the positive side of Olga's character and Rhoda must at least treat her with respect.

Catching Constance's eye, she said firmly,

'Olga has restyled her hair and settled for a more conventional appearance.'

'Not before time. She must be at least thirty.'

'Exactly thirty,' said Davenport. 'Quite young enough to make a fresh start.' It was clear he did not favour personal gossip about Olga and moved his guests to the dining-room, where Pixie tactfully started a new hare.

'And what of the famous diamond necklace? We heard the wildest rumours during our last few days in Madeira.' Davenport believed in simple facts as an antidote for gossip and narrated simply the story of the discovery of the necklace in the old communion box. He told it well while removing all sensational details and leaving them with the impression that the children alone were involved in the accidental breaking of the box.

'It happened the day of that dreadful fatal accident outside the English church didn't it?'

'Yes, that probably accounts for the wildness of the rumours.'

'The traffic in Funchal is appalling.' Constance stated the incontestable fact and Davenport did not comment.

'So there really was a diamond necklace,' said Pixie delightedly.

Rhoda recognised Pixie's positive quality in referring to the discovery rather than the fatality.

'It's a romantic story. I hope the church will benefit by it.'

The conversation passed into speculation of the necklace's monetary worth, to the Roscommons and their return to England and on to various recollections of Madeira omitting the traumatic events. In the impressions of sea, mountains and gardens, the true ambience of Madeira returned and the warm feeling that had promoted the dinner-party prevailed.

Over coffee and liqueurs, the disparate characters enjoyed companionship.

Who would have believed when we first met that we could in such a short time enjoy an evening together, Rhoda meditated. I thought Constance a tactless snob and Pixie a blundering do-gooder. I wonder what they thought of me?

She caught Matthew's eye and they smiled. He looked kindly at his other two guests having guessed Rhoda's thoughts from her speculative glance at them. When the taxi arrived for the ladies who were staying at a hotel in Oxford, they departed in amity. Beneath the surface and visible faults, they were united by a common faith and its values would override the superficial failings caused by class and environment.

Constance and Pixie were going home in the morning but Rhoda was staying longer to spend time with Davenport.

After the other guests had left, Rhoda and Matthew went to his college and sat in the fellows' garden in the wintry sunshine.

'Grant me earth's treats in Paradise to find,' Matthew quoted.

'Yes,' said Rhoda, 'if I ever accepted a visual image of heaven, it would be a garden. I am glad Alec was buried among the flowers of the British cemetery in Colonel Seaton's grave.'

Matthew nodded, 'I'm having an inscription added on the stone.'

They sat in silence for a time.

'I should think Napoleon's turning in his grave,' said Rhoda. 'I suppose the necklace *will* go to the English church?'

'Almost certainly. I hope Roscommon will get some of the proceeds for his parish. There is no doubt that the governor gave the box with no strings attached to the church well over a century ago.

Perhaps if Napoleon's sister, Pauline, had followed him into exile, it would have been returned to the family but she didn't. What an end for a man who had dominated Europe.'

'And what a fate for all the diamond necklaces he scattered round his family,' concluded Rhoda frivolously.

It was over a year later that Rhoda saw a headline outside a newsagent's shop, 'Surprise Sum for Napoleonic Necklace.' She bought a paper and read,

Recovered Treasure

The Last of Napoleon's Diamond Necklaces?

The last of Napoleon's gifts to his sisters was sold at Sotheby's for a million pounds. The buyer wishes to remain anonymous for security reasons but it is no secret that he is one of our newest multimillionaires.

It is ironic that this valuable treasure came to light by accident while two small boys were at play. Their parents have firmly refused an interview and wish to remain anonymous. Our readers will remember that before this embargo we published a photograph of the children, twin boys and a small sister. Our roving reporter happened to be chatting to parents waiting outside the school attended by these children and saw them as they came out. She ventured a question but the boys, firmly drilled at home no doubt, said, 'No comment' while the girl aimed a kick at our reporter's shins. Then the two boys seized either hand and dragged her off at the double. Though our reporter trotted alongside, no further word was spoken.

The purchase price is to be divided between the Church Urban Fund in Britain and an endowment of the English church in Madeira, where the necklace was discovered.

Our readers will doubtless wish to know why the government did not annex a large proportion of the money but our long-standing treaty with Portugal ensured that the matter was treated with unaccustomed tact. Whether the church is making the best use of this unexpected windfall is debatable. Should expatriates or those who, through their own inadequacies, cannot cope with modern society be recipients of more aid? A million pounds would be a handsome contribution to a new marina or recreation

166

centre for hardworking managers of our expanding economy. One wonders if the affair had gone to a court of appeal a different legal decision would have freed the money from the trammels of starry-eyed visionaries and misguided do-gooders?

Rhoda read no more and dropped the newspaper in a nearby recycling waste skip. On arriving home she rang up Matthew. In expressing delight at the worthwhile destination of the proceeds of the Napoleonic treasure, she exorcised the materialistic bigotry of the report. Matthew's equally unalloyed pleasure of the outcome was exhilarating. When she put down the phone she turned to the garden. All the delights of Madeira came back. The balmy air, the lavish blossom of flowers, the crocodiles of lively dark eyed children, the old fashioned courtesy of the mountain peasants, sunset over Reid's. Innumerable recollections of the Paradise Isle drifted before her eyes evoking magic like Flecker's in *Old Ships*:

It was so old a ship – who knows, who knows?
And yet so beautiful, I watched in vain
To see the mast burst open with a rose
And the whole deck put on its leaves again.